Miserations More

Mike Gutowski

Cover artwork created by Christine Filippou
For permission requests, contact the publisher, at:
Email: dadx3g@msn.com
Facebook: @mike.gutowski.62
softcover ISBN: 979-8-9873433-2-6
eBook ISBN: 979-8-9873433-3-3
Printed in the United States of America
Philosophy, Dark Fantasy, Dystopian Fantasy

First Edition

More rambles through the brambles of everyday life while searching for and experiencing the meaning of existence in the 21st century.

M.E.G. - - -

Introduction Untimely

What could be considered the end of this novella, I'm placing at the beginning. There's a method to this madness.

On Cosmology Theorems 10/02/2024 02:51 PM

Interesting thoughts fly amidst the human brain cells when contemplating the Universe concept. The substances of life likely exist for a time frame beyond our known sciences and terrestrial extant theories.

If a larger frame of time actually exists, then it must exist in a hypothetical box, but it then becomes plausible to exist as a box capable of holding an infinite number of sides, tops, and bottoms, such as boxes within boxes, etcetera. The known human mind has not yet figured out this puzzle paradox and, unfortunately, and somewhat randomly one day, the human mind may no longer exist able to solve the puzzle, or generate further contemplations. Perhaps a computer system will be invented capable of completing the randomness contemplation puzzle before human time runs out and into cosmological extinction.

Perhaps we are merely molecular and anatomical constructs herded like the spinning balls of a lottery game. Planet earth bound by mere accident and no more relevant or worthy of a standing on the dimensional stages of this or other universes than any of the other life forms. On earth these stages are built in many forms theoretical, biological, chemical, mechanical, political, subjective according to the creativity of the origin organisms available to and for the creation process. Creative creation, I suppose.

We form these concepts, in a way, fooling our mindful selves to logically posit and reconcile a purpose or meaning of life. Science, religion, political empires have all been rationally formatted according to these extant thinking processes. The missing puzzle pieces are filled in by creative thinking. The purpose? To promote continued survival. It could be concluded that humans and their philosophies of existence are just another form of entertainers on the live-action entertainment screen, cut and paste movie screen, or the printed words and pictures in literary works.

A biological entity seeks and competes for a space in the cosmos, subject to the constraints encountered and the existence form (predisposed physiology) inhabited. The human body form is a stage of its own, prancing and dancing about for to attain survival necessities and creatively wanted self-satisfaction, and sometimes for monetary remuneration or attention gratification. Simply put, "I exist, therefore I am". Whether existence is objectively realized, or not.

Summer Days More

On Success 06/29/2024 06:59 PM

Some people work hard and succeed. Some people work hard but remain douchebags.

Independence Day

On Mush Travels 07/04/2024 12:34 PM

Maybe I'm the last "natural writer" in the universe. AI is merely an amalgamation of mush. Mush is an easy and quick meal to cook. Keeps the human engine going. AI is similar. Going "where" is always the relevant question.

<u>On Social Constraints</u> 07/04/2024 12:41 PM

"Look at me. Look at me." Pretty much the essence of a human character trait. "I am. I'm here. Recognize who I am." Anonymity is a fear that rules all minds.

<u>On Car Productivity</u> 07/04/2024 05:41 PM

I'm guessing in the distant future that cars will become able to reproduce biologically. What kind of contraptions might result is anyone's guess.

<u>On Humans / Humanoids</u> 07/04/2024 09:40 PM

Once you figure out life, it becomes apparent it is a pretty sad mess. Are we the best we can be after thousands of trial-and-error years? Perhaps. We seem more like the rejects tossed out by a higher level of species civilization.

Independence Days More

<u>On Rulers and Gods</u> 07/05/2024 03:15 PM

Trust in a god serves the Ruler's purpose. Follow

the laws. Have faith in the god who created these laws. The Ruler uses these tenets as motivation leverage to rule. Declination of the "trust" is then considered rejection of the Ruler. And the Ruler exacts a price to be paid for such rejections. Governmental essence of this type poisons the air around this world.

On Murder Politics 07/08/2024 01:51 PM

When did this world become a place where popularity and acceptance depends upon which murderers one supports? Murderers of language, thoughts, reason, intellect, second guesses, perspective, numbers, letters, tumblers, feathers.

On Squat 07/08/2024 05:34 PM

Cat's out of the bag. Genie's out of the bottle. The fix is in again. All we can do is squattle.

Dark Times 07/10/2024 10:06 AM

(Sci-Fi story idea: "Dark Lands".)

If Einstein's theory is correct and time can be bent then it stands to reason it can also be broken. Then what? Do broken time threads and atom spewing time hoses flailing in varied parts of the universe exist? Broken atom hydrants? Is that possibility a reason to believe dark matter exists?

Climate Change 07/10/2024 10:44 AM

The fanatics pushing climate change ideology should more accurately be branded climate change "pushers". Selling an idea like selling drugs. No one wins in the long run. Hoping fleas are joyful about such inanity. The earth doesn't care.

On Life Requests 07/10/2024 12:39 PM

Forage for honest perspective and healthy criticism. Bountiful results abound.

On Seeing 07/11/2024 03:19 PM

Enlightenment stings the mind's eyes.

On Hope 07/12/2024 03:03 AM

Even false hope lives in the mind as an entity real.

On Human Propensities 07/12/2024 11:32 AM

We live in a world full of liars. No exceptions. Fare well or fall well.

On Facts 07/12/2024 06:58 PM

Facts are the glue that holds truth together.

On Storied Paths 07/14/2024 03:30 AM

Varied mysteries had eluded capture and resolution in his mind. A woman's lips, a man's voice, growth patterns of tree limbs, the moment triggering flight of a butterfly, a mantis turning of the head come to mind. The widest of mind experience mystery involved cologne. Sometimes the Mall stores located cologne departments near the exit. A means to attract patrons of any gender one last exploration attempt. Difficult to distinguish between a man versus woman scent.

On Life Sequences 07/16/2024 02:50 PM

Sometimes life will stream like a series of subsequent cruelties approaching a never end. They usually and eventually dissipate into a dead end. Another chance opportunity granted.

On Pushing Too Much 07/16/2024 11:12 PM

When people are pushed to the point where they have nothing to lose, then those who pushed them into this plight deserve to lose everything.

On Liberty and Freedom 07/16/2024 04:47 PM

USA Citizens were punished and terrorized this

much when King George III ruled this land.

<u>On Destiny</u> 07/17/2024 04:32 PM

The word "destiny" is sometimes used to fill in the logic and reason gaps a human mind is prone to block, for varied reasons, during extremely emotional and stressful events and time frames. The mind seeks to complete a confusing puzzle of life.

<u>On Personhood</u> 07/18/2024 12:27 PM

Humans can be hell. Humans can be heaven.

<u>On Scots</u> 07/18/2024 01:12 PM

When catching the eye of a Scottish woman, a mysterious energy overtakes your being.

<u>On Group Think</u> 07/18/2024 04:29 PM

On thing I've learned over years of working with and in groups. If they grow to not like you, it's because you're doing something right that they don't have the courage to admit, say, or do.

<u>On Understanding Government</u> 07/19/2024 02:30 PM

Who generally are highest paid workers in every so-called free or democratic countries? Government workers. Who hires the government workers? The politicians. Get it, yet?

On Government Bids 07/23/2024 06:57 PM

The government auctions off the lives of citizens to the highest bidders.

On Competence 07/23/2024 07:10 PM

Competence shines no color.

On Friends Reality 07/25/2024 12:07 PM

The family of friends is a sticky thought. A considerable number are committed to winning life's lottery. Back stabbers of smiling faces and happy demeanors abound.

On Want and Need 07/25/2024 02:36 PM

I hope you don't need much. An elevated level of want hurts much less than a small level of need.

On Death Anomalies 07/25/2024 02:46 PM

Humans are able to both mourn and celebrate life depending on the circumstances and culture extant.

On Necessity v. Necessary Spans 07/25/2024 02:50 PM

Not saying what necessarily is. Just saying what is necessary does.

On Planet Viability 07/25/2024 04:19 PM

Whether we need more or less people on earth has often been a question posed by scientist idiots. The earth doesn't care either way. It won't even exist a billion plus years from now.

On Politics 07/25/2024 04:19 PM

There exists only two primary political groups in much of the world: leftists and conservatives. All else are the mush in the middle.

On Writing Parameters 07/26/2024 02:15 AM

Sometimes writing is an attack on the mind. Sometimes it is a soothing back rub.

On Pursuit of Happiness 07/26/2024 02:31 AM

Finding yourself completely involves a lifelong search. Make it count. If chance will let you have it, you will not always search alone. On a most generous chance day perhaps can be discovered another person of a similar mindset. Such a joining of mindsets increases the chance of success. Many chances. Many failures. Many victories. Many successes may proceed during the mutual search.

<u>On Cemented Words</u> 07/26/2024 02:52 AM

When a person has words cemented into their brains for a long time, that person tends to dismiss layers of fresher cement.

<u>On Harmony</u> 07/26/2024 03:17 AM

When the mind and body work together then a rather glorious transformation becomes possible.

<u>On Yearbooks</u> 07/26/2024 04:25 AM

Looked through my college yearbook. Many memories in there, most of which stayed there.

<u>On New</u> 07/26/2024 02:09 PM

The crooks win. The innocent lose. What's new?

<u>On Brain Panning</u> 07/26/2024 11:59 PM

The human race, as currently constructed, seems to possess only two brain types. One type is sentient, rational, creative, critical thinkers. The other type is possessed of a garbage can brain sucking in all manner of marketing, pseudo educational, and political propaganda used to make best guess decisions. Decisions are sometimes the best guess and least guess propositions. One bodes well for humanity. The other bodes poorly as imminent and ultimate destruction.

Dead Man Imaginations 07/27/2024 03:26 AM

(Story Idea)

An old man dies. When a neighbor checks on him, has to use spare key given to him by the man. The neighbor goes in, notices odd, rank smell. Looks around the house, finds bare accouterments, small couch, hassock, cocktail table, a few paintings prints of unknown artists each signed "unknown". Described oddness of paintings of always a shadow figure in distance at different scenes, in rain, sun, gray days, snow.

Finally, on the second-floor secrets are revealed, boxed but unopened sex tools, and some Knick knacks on a dresser top, and a box. The shadow comes out of the box and creates a mischief dance along the walls. The shadow transforms itself into the shadow displayed in each painting. Other mysteries have yet to be revealed.

On Door Knockers 07/27/2024 02:28 PM

When someone unexpected knocks at the door, don't immediately open it. A phrase to rebuff their sales intimidation tactics or nefarious intentions actions sounds as follows: "I will show you to hell, but I'm sure you already know where it is located." Scratch that. Or better yet, don't answer the door knock. A negated sales person may then resort to nefarious actions. Or maybe they will leave an advertising leaflet.

On Voting Hyperbole 07/27/2024 03:19 PM

Asking people to vote their conscience sounds a bit banal. Too many people wouldn't know a conscience if it stung them in the ass.

On Visitors 07/27/2024 03:51 PM

Short and sweet and get out of town helps the host avoid a frown.

On Christians 07/28/2024 01:15 AM

Christians have known what persecution feels like

for over 2,000 years. Name a deadly sin. It has been committed against them. Disrespect for their very being is somewhat known at birth. Still, they persist in a mission for serenity. See Redux 09/05/2024.

On Data Collection 07/28/2024 03:00 AM

Lies, damned lies, and government statistics.

On Journalism 07/28/2024 01:15 PM

It remains difficult to tell a truth story when much effort goes into sweeping facts under the rug. A dusty and dirty business.

Wedding Toast 07/28/2024 07:57 PM

May life greet you with a big wet kiss . . . wherever or whenever it may be needed.

On Life Travels 07/28/2024 08:00 PM

8 PM on planet earth, still navigating the cause and causes ways.

On Government Corruption 07/29/2024 11:47 AM

A corrupt government makes the rules of reality, imposes them upon citizens, but doesn't apply the same rules upon themselves.

On Political Real Estate 07/29/2024 12:49 PM

The way some political parties operate, it could be deduced they've already bought condominiums in Hell.

On Politicians 07/29/2024 02:44 PM

Eternal and infamous squatters.

Three Hoaxes 07/29/2024 02:44 PM

Climate Change Hysterics, Political Justice, Cryptocurrency.

On Government Civility 07/29/2024 02:58 PM

A Dr. Seussian nightmare, like green eggs and spam; green dregs and scam; the ritz and the twits; Dorkin' meets a Coup; Sham I Am; totalitarian we must . . . .

On Politics Drug Abuse 07/29/2024 09:54 PM

Our politicians have overdosed on a drug called Power. Drunk on power is a situation dour.

On Big Tech Drunkenness 07/29/2024 10:02 PM

The Big Tech companies are stone cold drunk on

sips of their own power. They seem to think they are invincible. Remarkably close to a label of intellectual terrorists.

On Political Spins 07/29/2024 10:39 PM

When does politics stop the destruction from statues to statutes.

On Presidential Politics 07/30/2024 02:41 PM

After Kamala is installed as President we'll be burning bibles to stay warm.

Migraines – Horror Story 07/30/2024 03:38 PM

An 11-year-old boy suffers a horrible migraine at his grandma's house. He is given medicine to cause sleep so he can suffer less pain, but he can still hear grandparents speaking during the mind buzzing pain. They are worried about him but are worried this migraine curse has been genetically passed down to their grandson. Could mean ruin for them, him, and the neighborhood, because when the buzzing gets louder, human and structure destruction ensues.

On Government Truths 07/31/2024 03:05 PM

A government that placates citizens with lies is a government bent on citizen destruction.

On Elections Corrupt 08/01/2024 11:09 AM

Biden has coddled our enemies and terrorized our citizens.

On Stupid 08/01/2024 01:42 PM

Stupid people will insist their stupidity be accepted, and further, recognized as achievement that "requires" a grand life woefully unearned.

On Safe Harbors 08/01/2024 02:14 PM

Corruption has even affected the Olympics. At this point, doom needs no safe harbor. At this point it is moored in all harbors.

On Governments 08/01/2024 02:28 PM

Governments are pathological liars lying pathologically.

On Self Identity 08/01/2024 03:02 PM

Apparently, now, we can identify as any race, color, creed, religion, or biological fantasy we choose.

On Audience Protocol 08/01/2024 04:39 PM

A well-practiced spectator can better appreciate the show.

On Debauchery Speeding 08/01/2024 05:58 PM

In the pantheon of human desires, debauchery never rests at a solid red traffic signal.

On Wellness 08/01/2024 06:03 PM

All some humans need is a beer and a smoke. A cheap date. PS: Some humans no longer date.

On Humanity Eclipse 08/02/2024 01:29 AM

Any convergence of dreams and reality acts as a human mind eclipse.

On Beauty 08/02/2024 02:09 PM

Beauty carries many expressions in the perspective barrel. Love is one of those expressions.

On Post Covid Tastes 08/02/2024 02:36 PM

Chocolate chips never betray the taste buds.

On Human Creature Traits 08/02/2024 03:15 PM

We are all scavengers seeking the safest moment to strike.

Everything Nothing 08/03/2024 12:39 PM

A man is tired of being picked on by people in his town. He moved to this town called Contentment to relax and live out the waning days of his life. The town turned out to be not as advertised. The townspeople didn't know he possessed the power to dissolve everything into nothing at his whim.

On Humans 08/03/2024 02:14 PM

Pretty simple. Every one of them hides a monster of varied capabilities deep inside of them just waiting to break out. The purpose of the break out depends on the necessity of the situation. Purposes noble to nefarious rest along the consciousness spectrum.

On Memories 08/03/2024 11:03 PM

Over time, the human mind becomes calloused over by real grief moments as a self-protection mechanism, then, magically the good memories occasionally roar back into the happy previously shared moments. Some tilting of the vision occurs along the memory path.

On Hell, Heaven 08/04/2024 12:58 PM

(see Thomas Hobbs, philosopher)

If Hell is truth seen too late, then is Heaven truth seen too early? Does perceived truth stunt the search effort for discovery of further truth?

<u>On Circus Politics Puzzles</u> 08/04/2024 01:16 PM

Four more years of a one ring circus or four new years of a three-ring circus. A puzzling dilemma.

<u>On Collapse Structural</u> 08/04/2024 02:36 PM

The Olympics, journalism, and democracy are dead. 21st Century moments of collapse dread.

<u>On Reality Boxing</u> 08/05/2024 02:49 PM

To understand the common human, an understanding of everyday life creatures is essential. Revelations remain a mystery for those reluctant to pursue a firm grasp of reality and truth. Most schools from top to bottom fear teaching truth because it would expose their own nefarious intentions. The modern-day schooling intentions revolve around a pounding of mantras and musts forbidden to deviate from. Call it anything politically that can be imagined, but in reality it is a method of uncompromising indoctrination. A perfect means to undermine a proper societal functionality down to the last standing brick.

<u>On Theories</u> 08/05/2024 03:55 PM

Theory acts much like a garbage can. Sews up a lot of thoughts sometimes disposable.

<u>On Questions</u> 08/05/2024 04:30 PM

Who frames the question designs the expected answer.

<u>On Worldview</u> 08/05/2024 07:12 PM

Life has a worldwide meaning and citizens would

like to live it that way from their own personal perspectives, and not live only from the perspective of serving politicians. Politics is a dirty business, a world prone to turning upside down in a heartbeat, driven by corruption. That world doesn't take kindly to either living or dying, or whether it matters at all.

<u>On Nightmares</u> 08/07/2024 02:16 AM

Some people have nightmares and never seem to know why. They read books on dream interpretation. Still, the reason or reasons why haunting nightmares persist provides no resolution personal.

On Body Mutilation 08/07/2024 02:22 AM

(Story Idea)

Young children are taken by teachers and transported to secret medical facilities where they are surgically mutilated against their will. As adults they form a secret society dedicated to tracking down and punishing the mutilators, by mutilating them.

On Perspective 08/07/2024 10:21 AM

How does a child living in poverty view their environment? Similarly, how does a President or Prime Minister view their environment?

Puberty's Revenge 08/07/2024 05:24 PM

(Story Idea)

Minors drugged up with puberty blockers revolt. Intended revenge rage victims = parent(s), teachers, medical doctors and nurses, NIH Federal, State, County, Township and other government agencies, purveyors of child abuse.

On RX's and Sanity 08/07/2024 05:29 PM

Media journalism is totally loco. They must take loco pills every day of the week.

On Government Agencies 08/7/2024 06:09 PM

If you're 50 years old or older, there isn't a single one of you that hasn't suffered the oppression of a local, city, state, or federal government agency. Poorly trained managers produce poorly minded workers. (See also: workers of corporations and small businesses)

On Government Math 08/07/2024 07:25 PM

Government spending agencies seem quite unable to properly herd the monetary ones and zeros.

On Political Environments 08/08/2024 02:48 PM

There exists totalitarian States and there exists totalitarian worlds. Earth now fits the "worlds" category, quite neatly, and the puzzle has almost reached completion.

On Reality Pickles 08/08/2024 3:02 PM

In order to address reality, one must address reality. "Reality, how are you today?" Answers to such a general question may not immediately become forthcoming. Only time and a taut, concerted intellectual effort helps birth fruits and flowers to ripen and bloom.

On Politicians 08/28/2024 10:47 PM

Politicians are good at 2 things: hoodwinking and bamboozling.

On American Freedoms 08/09/2024 12:02 PM

Americans live generally homogeneous in purpose, but in means and measures live as a hodgepodge of tastes and fancies.

On Socializing 08/09/2024 12:22 PM

It used to be pretty faces that affected my thought process, but with age and experience, what's been found to inhabit the minds of any faces makes or breaks the tolerability of pursuing and maintaining a relationship.

On Knowledge Costs 08/09/2024 12:25 PM

Knowledge is cheap. Using it is expensive.

On Politics Anomalies 08/09/2024 12:32 PM

Corruption is a major skill in the political parties.

The choice is one of more corruption against less corruption. The party with the most followers benefiting from corruption tends to win.

<u>On Immigration</u> 08/09/2024 12:37 PM

Politicians illegally import more potential voters to replace the numbers of voters their policies killed.

<u>On Media Communications</u> 08/09/2024 02:11 PM

Lies are hidden in the telling of facts. Observe and analyze the motivations of major and lesser media company communications behind the scenes and directly released to the public. The clues are more than obvious.

<u>On Poetry</u> 08/09/2024 02:43 PM

News is farce. Perspectives worse. Living and dying under the politics curse.

<u>On Misinformation Squabbles</u> 08/08/2024 08:33 PM

Perhaps one person's truth is another person's misinformation. Letting the government decide the issue is akin to societal suicide.

On Simple Starts 08/09/2024 09:17 PM

A dot's worth of energy is the starting point of any illumination, rumination, or stimulation.

On Battered Memories 08/10/2024 03:43 AM

I miss who you were and to this day the memories sting in a random blur.

On Normal 08/10/2024 11:56 PM

Humans in the 21st century have changed the meaning of normal. All that was considered weird is normal. All that was considered normal is weird.

On Literary License 08/10/2024 11:58 PM

Huxley wrote of a brave new world. Orwell wrote of a 1984. Every year now is a bit of both.

On Aging 08/12/2024 12:08 AM

Time offers no guarantees. It passes steady for all whether ready or weary.

On Loving Poetry 08/12/2024 01:19 AM

That feeling right here in my heart, for you. It never goes away in hue. Never truly wanes. Even though we've gone our separate ways, the feeling remains.

Will never go away. I don't even try to let if flee on its own volition any longer. No fences remain for it to jump or break down. No longer does my mind play me for a clown. It lives as nature intended. Fences mended.

<u>On Competition</u> 08/12/2024 01:36 PM

Winning hurts and losing hurts. Choose your hurt.

<u>On Extremes</u> 08/12/2024 04:26 PM

Silence is not golden. Silence is death.

<u>On New Communication Rules</u> 08/12/2024 04:47 PM

Truth and justice are no longer a "fine" or "fashionable" thing. 21st century language, aka mis-language rules are under siege by and from worldwide elites. We must be kept in the dark because their light is too bright for us. A shady and dim parody of rules, and too, the elites. The elites are enlightened, or are they just lit poorly.

<u>On Human Futility</u> 08/12/2024 08:52 PM

Humans never seem to run out of ways to sabotage their own societal best interests.

<u>On Societal Chaos</u> 08/12/2024 09:06 PM

There really is no society as a whole and consistent mindset anymore unless it has been brutally crushed and pressed into the service of bowing to the committee rulers. It is a series of societies being stirred around in a mixing bowl. Many of the free world countries lay infected by many rules written and assumed, intentionally afflicted by elites and politicians. Leaders promote chaos in order to hold their power firm. Who controls the spoon, or the electric mixer, controls the societal functions.

<u>On Sounds Peaceful</u> 08/12/2024 09:20 PM

There is no silence at night as creatures alight. There is no silence at daybreak as creatures awake. There is no silence at noon as creatures aswoon.

<u>On Societal Sentience</u> 08/12/2024 11:34 AM

Humans never cease to run out of ways to sabotage their own societies.

<u>On Government How</u> 08/13/2024 03:29 PM

It is a universal tenet that governments eventually destroy their populace if given enough time to operate in such a manner. World history proves the point. Some governments become reformed under the force of citizen revolts. Some dissolve as they run out of money and resources forcibly taken. No exceptions.

<u>On Hounds' Time</u> 08/13/2024 03:31 PM

It's the thirteenth day of the thirteenth month and none of the hounds can be kept at bay.

<u>On Fear Benefits</u> 08/13/2024 03:57 PM

Scared of failure is a human necessity since fear helps assist creation of many mechanical objects which further human evolution capability.

<u>On Animal Farms Speak</u> 08/13/2024 06:31 PM

"We get a chance to live. Another day to last. We get a chance to live, and utter one more laugh. Better to laugh than die. Better to breathe than cry. Wonder isn't the game. Wander eating, the same."

<u>On Mind Wanderings</u> 08/13/2024 06:37 PM

Just trying to be witty, not shitty. Okay, sometimes shitty is needed.

<u>On Time</u> 08/13/2024 09:03 PM

Time is an existence emission regulated facetiously

by the government. And the universe doesn't care.

On Media Self-Adulation 08/14/2024 02:51 AM

The noble journalist has evolved into a myth. Noble journalists don't tell lies with impunity. Such circumstances mock the audience of readers; sows little sense of the queer perspectives in which the audience views them. The view, from the audience, beams a light of ignorance, and the source of that light is journalism teachers. Indoctrinators of how to tell a ready and readable mischaracterization of brutal life realities.

On Passions Betrayal 08/14/2024 03:25 AM

Betray a little. Betray a lot. The degree of betrayal steams the pot.

On Drink Mixes 08/14/2024 02:21 PM

What drink mixes well with a spritz of betrayal?

On Ant Terrorism 08/14/2024 02:30 PM

While sittin' on the bathroom shitter I noticed many ants of the latest litter zeroing in on recently laid poison traps cautiously at first, then spreading their troops outward from the trap locations in lines viewed as sun rays beaming. The traps seemed insufficiently bitter enough to coax many of the tiny terrorists into a suffering of total annihilation. Even the tiled wailing walls behind and to the left of the shitter observed the shenanigans but dismissed my urgent fears of a mission failure. A truce remains less a possibility while hags and drones inhabiting the interiors of wall spaces groan for death in totality. Invasions at other locations in kitchen, pantry, and mudroom have also commenced with similar defensive measures applied. Results are still uncertain.

<u>On Big Tech Machinations</u> 08/14/2024 06:28 PM

The Big Tech companies share a common bond. They are the most prevalent and massive misinformation, disinformation, and propaganda purveyors across the globe. Readings of many ancient paper bound books tends to soften the blows of these intellect attacks.

<u>Freak on Freak</u> 08/15/2024 03:50 AM

(Story Idea)

The earth is a laboratory for creations of hybrid killers comprised of all human, humanoid, animal creatures species and sub-species. Each are hybrids long swimming in the same gene pools collectively. The freaks inhabiting the pool are called in, out, and up, pressed into battle service. They've been bred into beings of unquenchable hungers and thirsts.

When ordered, essentially activated, the killing never stops on the battlefield or other locations they are called to fight upon. Some are bred to work quietly, almost silently, mimicking the natural attack location sounds so as not to spook the chosen prey. These soldiers could spray from their mouths aroma intoxication scents like Ginger as means to slow and pacify the instinctual senses of attack targets.

Special freak forces included Hardheads, essentially a battering ram of metal plated head possessing cheetah speed.

Indoctrinators, a mix of humans and humanoids served also in Special freak forces as hypnotizers using words to lure enemy forces into inevitable doom situations.

Doc Fiz, a mix of humans and humanoids served

as medical doctors specializing in physics and mechanics theory. Their purpose was to maintain and repair as necessary any freaks deemed out of sync with their inner selves; helped to realign freak skill sets and keep each in balance.

In battle, only the sounds of bone breaks and flesh tears changed the quieter edges of audible harmony. To date, every Freak force mission has resulted in an "all targets eliminated" conclusion. Efficient, swift, deadly. ESD events. Nicknamed: Freak dances.

Temperature and weather factors affected skilled quality. Generally, more heat meant better energy displacement and skill control, but excess heat conditions resulted in depletion of energy. Colder temperatures slowed skill sets and set them into defense shield mode. Chilling served a purpose of allowing the freak mechanisms to regenerate. Day shade and cool nights assisted the process. Portable and mobile Chillers of human, humanoid, and machine units accompanied all missions.

On Idiot Bashing Day 08/16/2024 01:19 PM

We really need a "Fuck You Idiots" Friday on

Twitter/X every now and then, maybe once a month like on the full moon. No harm intended in this endeavor. All of us need to acknowledge, no matter how smart or otherwise we've been deemed, we still possess moments of complete and sometimes earth-shattering idiocy.

On Voting 08/16/2024 01:57 PM

I don't vote for thieves. I need the money more than they need the money.

Socialist Definition 08/16/2024 02:02 PM

Those people and politicians who demand your earned resources while you wish to keep, dispense them according to your own discretion.

On Hippy Mantras 08/16/2024 02:18 PM

Remember the saying "go along to get along"? Yeah. Many a community or business venture has suffered catastrophic destruction following this entrenched mindset.

On Government Spending 08/16/2024 02:33 PM

Maybe it's time to hire some spray painters nationwide to spread the words: "Government

Spending is Death".

On Civilization Viability 08/16/2024 09:09 PM

A population of one mind pure becomes powerful, yet that population becomes frozen in time. A one purpose culture moves onward in slow and steady degrees. A culture of one mind leads to degradation and destruction. It becomes unable to discern dangers and change needs.

On Socialism 08/17/2024 03:13 AM

When you need ID for every purchase of anything, but not for voting. Now that's a kick in the pants, pantsuits, wallet, and purse.

On Group Thoughts 08/17/2024 05:30 PM

The puzzlers puzzled so much their puzzle became broken.

On Life Living 08/17/2024 05:44 PM

Living a life short of everything needed to prosper on a daily basis is the usual circumstance of the human animal at large.

On Speech Freedoms 08/17/2024 06:30 PM

Free speech is cherished by the populace masses

which is exactly why their governments fear and despise the concept.

On Governance by Fiat 08/17/2024 10:57 PM

A democracy eventually kills two birds with one stone: republics and socialisms. What's left when the dust clears are simply communist societies.

On Late Night TV 08/18/2024 03:01 PM

Gibberish and hornswoggle no longer sells.

On Love and More 08/18/2024 11:04 PM

Humans have developed concepts meant to help

them fit into and understand society, ergo love and religion and politics, all of which exist as essential fictions. Really just a song of jagged harmony.

On Telling Oneself Falsehoods 08/19/2024 02:04 PM

Those who have no shame find it difficult to display their own shame.

On Socialism Values 08/19/2024 02:16 PM

No value in socialism exists. It is the opposite of a citizen controlled free market economy. A sign of paranoia plagues politicians. They simply and regularly don't trust the people they were elected to represent. Trillions of dollars in added deficit spending betray a truth. Good service is wanting.

On Social Meetings 08/19/2024 05:12 PM

To make friends involves numerous exploratory caveats. Attending drinking establishments or even a friend's residence is a somewhat helpful means of socializing, but still, caveats apply. The caveats are revealed during the linguistic journey at each location.

On Defiance Quotients 08/19/2024 11:13 PM

The limits of defiance defines the perspective measure of the human mind.

On Political Words 08/20/2024 01:31 PM

Pelosied: figurative language meaning stabbed in

the back while whispering sweet nothings. Synonyms: Bidened, Schumered, Clintoned, Obamaed, Riced.

On Truth Digs 08/20/2024 04:31 PM

Truth has many times been revealed much like an

archaeological dig discovery. Scratch and dig repeatedly until truth reveals itself. Brush the dust away and learn its intricacies. Truth generally had been buried in ancient (modern times meaning is a bit more than a few years ago) perspectives and viewpoint vantages. When thoroughly cleaned off, it gleams.

On Truth Uses 08/20/2024 04:46 PM

Truth is a weapon. Perspective is a shield.

On Politics Monsters 08/21/2024 01:32 PM

What kind of totalitarian monster imposes taxes on unrealized gains? Oh, we know now. And when we know, the TMs (totalitarian monsters) consider us house slaves who know too much, worthy of their persecution.

On Politics Puzzles 08/21/2024 02:05 PM

Citizens know well how the puzzle pieces fit together. Underestimating their sentience is the downfall of many monsters.

On Word Mixes 08/21/2024 02:20 PM

Words have meaning whether we like it or not.

On Screamers 08/21/2024 02:42 PM

Screaming tends to exacerbate the deemed problems a screamer would prefer to disappear.

On Knowledge Searches 08/21/2024 03:20 PM

Seeking knowledge is many times a mission bereft of charity, and so too, clarity.

On Politics Salad 08/21/2024 04:31 PM

Crook and idiot isn't a good combination for a Caeser's Salad.

On Human Rights 08/21/2024 04:46 PM

An individual exists supreme over a government.

On Pain Fitness 08/21/202405:32 PM

Pain serves as a barometer for physical, emotional, or intellectual limits. Each of these endurance categories can be exceeded using caution. The goal is to live fit enough to live tomorrow.

On Government and Citizen Responsibility 08/22/2024 05:46 PM

Governments have regularly proven they can't be trusted. Citizens need to take responsibility for the failures of their governments. Only next rational solutions can be considered, approved, and implemented.

<u>On Drones Political</u> 08/22/2022 06:06 PM

The citizens and their markets are perfectly capable of determining what's fair. We refuse and don't need the help of any politician to make that decision for us. Politicians are our drones. We can turn them off at our own discretion.

<u>On Political Conventions</u> 08/22/2024 07:12 PM

Watching a political convention is like watching paint dry. At least the painted wall eventually dries.

<u>On Life Mysteries</u> 08/22/2024 07:29 PM

I've had a conversation with life many times, or tried to do so. It is either a poor listener or I'm just reluctant to embrace the mysteries revealed.

<u>On People Interactions</u> 08/23/2024 03:13 PM

Many people calculate the ration, emotionally of how many others can appreciate a style, spoken language pattern, or social interaction pattern appropriate for acceptance. Whoever decides to run the race risks a poor finish. That's just life.

On 21st Century Election Cycles 08/23/2024 03:32 PM

Honestly, a quite unexpected surprise in this weirdest of Election campaign cycles but perhaps expected in this most unique Big Tech carpet bombed 2lst century. (see RFK, Jr endorsement of former President Trump)

On A Political Press 08/23/2024 04:15 PM

Many of the news press and journalism communities have committed mass political coverage suicide. A condition they've pursued for many years. Don't mourn their demise in the least. It is well-earned.

On Faith 08/24/2024 11:24 PM

Political faith is worn like a threadless leisure jacket.

On Media 08/24/2024 11:47 PM

The leftists pretty much own and work for the major media. Truth in most avenues of news and opinion broadcasting is a ghost chasing the wind.

On Delusions 08/25/2024 12:13 AM

Beware the human ignorance of intellectual shortcomings and intentions.

On Legal Vote Verification 08/25/2024 12:24 AM

A citizen who rejects the idea and purpose of voter identity verification supports nefarious and unaccountable voting methods.

On Remembering Politicians 08/25/2024 01:08 AM

Some politicians are remembered for greatness. Some politicians are remembered for bleakness. Some citizens don't seem to know the difference.

Biology vs. Gender Wars 08/25/2024 01:28 AM

Biology = man, woman; male, female.

Gender = he-man, she-man, she-woman, he-woman.

A dichotomy categorization of natural life, and artificial life, promoted by chaos mongers and social scientists. *Social science is not much science.

Old school thoughts: Big Tech makes the clay; Social scientists mold it. Pretty simple.

On Bolshevik Life 08/25/2024 01:36 AM

We've pretty much all portrayed ourselves as Bolsheviks at some narcissistic or nihilistic point in our own lives. From grade school to doctorate pursuits. For some the mindset dissipates faster than a morning fog. For some, the fog never lifts, haunting the mind.

On Politicking 08/25/2024 01:49 AM

The politicians have evolved into a semi-retired and time-doddering bunch of old fools and young fools, devoid of a sense common, responsibility and self-examination be damned. They've become so translucent in actions that we can see right through them. Propaganda media hides such truths as if that action can make reality disappear.

On Destiny's Foundation 08/25/2024 12:44 PM

A name doesn't matter. Beliefs do. Actions reveal.

On Prejudice 08/25/2024 12:51 PM

A corrupt government makes the rules of reality

and imposes them upon citizens, but doesn't apply those rules to themselves.

On Weddings 08/25/2024 06:57 PM

What we remember today reminds us of yesterday. Especially at special moments in time.

On Citizen Fishing 08/26/2024 11:10 AM

Politicians bait their citizen fishing hooks with worms designed to attract verbalized opinions for capture. By this means, politicians determine who will become a target for destruction.

On Speech Phobia 08/26/2024 11:32 AM

Free speech and Hate speech each qualify as speech. In today's world, any word or word combination can be classified as either depending on a listener's perspective. A slippery slope if ever one existed.

On the 21st Century 08/26/2024 01:56 PM

It is a century like any other century in one respect. Trust misplaced is self-destructive.

On Pursuits 08/27/2024 04:54 AM

What gets you going starts the engine of knowing.

On Outer Space Territory 08/27/2024 04:18 PM

Outer Space "territory" will work just like earth lands and seas. Countries will try to occupy it and claim it as their own domain, then those same countries will place restrictions and charge fees for other countries to heed before entry is allowed. Another war trap.

On Government Tolerance 08/27/2024 04:33 PM

It is in the nature of governments to impose fees and liberty penalties upon citizens and visitors with whom the governments disagree.

On False Dictates 08/27/2024 04:43 PM

We are born with original sin, racism, and a propensity to lie traits. There is no factual evidence of these originality traits. This "original" concept is a hoax.

On Writing Perspective 08/27/2024 09:24 PM

I no longer pray. I poet.

On Interpretation 08/28/2024 02:41 PM

Reality shapes the mind, but reality can be falsified

or mimicked. False reality has taken hold like a plague permanent.

<u>On Inspiration</u> 08/28/2024 02:48 PM

The artwork of family and friends has greatly inspired the writing of words which now inhabit many books.

<u>On Aspiration</u> 08/28/2024 02:50 PM

Another day cycle completed. Another day cycle in progress. Another day cycle future tempts the fates.

<u>On Hell's Heaven</u> 08/28/2024 02:57 PM

If hell is truth seen too late (Thomas Hobbs) then heaven must be a sentient serene state.

<u>On Universal Wishes</u> 08/28/2024 03:00 PM

Greatest wish for humankind: a heaven is found.

<u>On Woke-A-Dope Policy</u> 08/28/2024 04:15 PM

Justice is a two-way mirror long ago shattered. An ugly simple.

<u>On Sense Debilitation</u> 08/28/2024 07:14 PM

Believe your senses. They tend to warn of real

danger. Which reminds us why drug manufacturers are so prominent in our lives. Drugs tend to dull the senses. Control the mind, control the body.

On Government Utility 08/29/2024 01:48 PM

The government is a business as corrupt as can be imagined.

On Leadership Corrosion 08/29/2024 01:52 PM

If you have to fight and protest your government to preserve your individual freedoms, then you've chosen the wrong leaders.

On Corporate and Government Needs 08/29/2024 01:56 PM

Businesses and governments die under the weight and auspices of slackers and patronage hires.

On Gov Sins 08/29/2024 02:20 PM

The wages of government incompetence loom broad and long.

On Work and Leisure Parody 08/29/2024 04:52 PM

What doesn't kill us kills us eventually.

On Politics and Elections 08/29/2024 05:08 PM

Some politicians seem to think cheating us out of our constitutional rights is their constitutional right.

On 21st Century Politics 08/29/2024 06:32 PM

Whatever politician can promise to steal away money from honest citizens and redistribute it to loyalist voters generally wins the political game.

On Fast-Food Training 08/29/2024 08:02 PM

Every young worker should experience, even once if briefly, the fast-food industry process and how it teaches the responsibility of Teamwork and daily dedication to the assigned tasks. Somewhat similar to military training but not as physically, mentally rigorous or stressful.

On Education Choices 08/29/2024 08:31 PM

Parents are education consumers. If they find a product that doesn't satisfy their needs, they can choose to buy from another seller in the same market. Making choices isn't a war tactic. Public education isn't a monopoly.

On Certainty 08/29/2024 10:49 PM

In the Age of the Big Tech teacher lives a cruel certainty.

On War Tactics 08/30/2024 05:20 PM

If you look at every problem like a war in progress then you will shoot yourself in the foot.

On the Nature of Creatures and Humans 08/31/2024 03:28 AM

The essence of nature is merciless. It cannot be reasoned with. The essence of humans is not dissimilar.

On Religion Understanding 08/31/2024 01:44 PM

The major cultural difference between a few religions is how they treat disobedient women. Most religions have banned inhumane practices many ages ago.

On Outer Space Wonders 08/31/2024 02:25 PM

Sometimes it seems we are ground ants wondering if spiders really exist.

On Skid Quests 08/31/2024 04:57 PM

The quest in Skid Row Nation leads to a destination of unpredictable origin. Skid cautious.

<u>On Propaganda</u> 09/01/2024 11:43 AM

"The Purpose of Propagandists is to make one set of people forget that certain other sets of people are human." – Aldous Huxley

<u>On Politician Skill Declines</u> 09/01/2024 08:55 PM

Minimum skill requirements for a politician should include screw in, and out a light bulb; public speaking competence; balance a financial budget. Skill tests should be required yearly.

<u>On Vote Cheating</u> 09/01/2024 09:09 PM

If it doesn't make sense then it doesn't make sense. Why would voters continue to vote into office politicians who lie, cheat, and steal from them? It doesn't make sense.

<u>On Matters Unconscionable</u> 09/01/2024 09:26 PM

Why do politicians prefer protective fences circling around their own houses, property borders, and work spaces, including Identification credentials, at the access points, then refuse to grant the same protections at the Election voting precincts. Something crooked a citizen's way comes.

On Liberation and Crony Governments 09/01/2024 09:50 PM

Far too many places on this planet are bugged up by some corrupt and insane politicians. Perhaps they mirror some of the citizens who voted for them. The administrative machines of many governments seem poisoned beyond relief. Only one conclusion can be drawn.

On Class Communication 09/01/2024 09:57 PM

A rich human and a poor human stand next to each other. A rare possibility, true. A conversation is a possibility. Does it happen? Rarely.

On Government Vacancy 09/01/2024 10:13 PM

After learning of the terrorist murders of 6 Israeli captured citizens including 1 USA dual citizen held against their will in hostile territory, I can't help but wonder what in the hell is wrong with the USA government leaders. The White House appears physically, morally, and socially vacant. Maybe that's because the White House has been available for sale to the highest bidder over the last 4 years. Unconscionable.

Labor Day

On Conversation Circles 09/02/2024 04:39 AM

When the last word is also the first word then the conversation is over.

On Book Titles 09/02/2024 05:51 AM

"Strike" = impact, or = swung baseball bat missed contact upon the pitched ball, or = labor – end/deny work production.

Characters: Len (Lender of money ideas); Amat (creative theoretician, pretender); PH (spender of time and money, name means short for PHD who never completed studies)

On Nature Feats 09/02/2024 06:17 PM

All things never stop moving, from atoms to molecules to weather conditions to outer space entities to planetary creatures, trees, plants upon, under, or extant in oceans and waterways. Existence doesn't stop. Perhaps it was designed that way. Not a nonsense dance. A dance of purpose.

Labor Days More

On Writing More 09/03/2024 01:58 PM

Writing involves finding mind thoughts, then putting them to clever use.

On Writing 09/03/2024 02:19 PM

Sometimes while writing my brain surprises me. Thank you, brain.

On Repeats Appetite 09/03/2024 02:34 PM

Good vibes, like good times, do regenerate like a McDonald's, Taco Bell, Chicken-fil-A, Popeyes, Burger King, IHOP, Domino's, Pizza Hut, KFC, or Wendy's menu.

On Government Honesty 09/03/2024 02:41 PM

Assets have gone the way of a dodo bird. Liabilities have multiplied like summer's flies. A divorce seems necessary.

On Social Query 09/03/2024 02:49 PM

Query whether religions or sports have saved and

enhanced more lives during the modern era of human history. An answer, upon first look, isn't obvious. The balance sheet of assets, liabilities, and capital is incomplete, historically.

<u>On Sound Timing Usefulness</u> 09/03/2024 02:53 PM

Many songs started by loud shouts of sound voices or musical notes boom out inspiring. Many conversations originating from loud voice shouts begin dead in the inspiration waters.

<u>On Dead End Profits</u> 09/03/2024 03:54 PM

A dead end opens the mind to enhanced ingenuity. A live end of electricity needs a safe cap.

<u>On Sounds and Thoughts Unknown</u> 09/04/2024 04:15 AM

Mysterious sounds. Strange lights. Hauntings of the dark pre-dawn brights. Hags and crones throwing stones, or maybe a mouse seeking exit below the floor boards Sleeping naught amidst the moment's sound hoards. A doomsday look of Hallum's Alomes.

<u>On Life Moments</u> 09/04/2024 01:45 PM

If a whole life is lived, and a few significant success moments were achieved during the process, then a life well-lived has occurred.

On Gobble Dee Gook 09/04/2024 03:11 PM

When wisdom becomes garbled during translation. Wisdom shared, whether later deemed useful or not so, serves a purpose temporary. Thinking rationally helps.

On Baloney Talkers 09/04/2024 04:12 PM

People who talk like they have a slice of baloney in their mouth may actually have a slice of baloney in their mouth.

On Generational Organized Crime 09/05/2024 11:28 AM

Basically, there's trivial difference between a terrorist group and government politicians. Each finds a means to suppress the will of the citizenry. Any place. Any time. By any means. From petty theft to murder. A media outlet, usually working for one or the other of oppressive entities, pulls down the shades so as not to expose the charade. Citizens exist amongst seas of crimes / criminals.

Examples below.

Movie Makers: they portray every illness and crime imaginable. Essentially mimicking grim societal realities. Fantasy love stories are salted and peppered into the respective perspective mixes to soften the viewers sensory tastebuds.

Governments: much has been written in many literary genres about corrupt governments and their structural operation methods. Generally, there exists secret agencies which monitor citizen activity. Reports of this activity are provided to political leaders. Those leaders, outside of the usual scrutiny processes and protections legally extant, take measures to suppress citizen activity that lessens the effect of criminal activity which the politicians benefit from. The citizens who best play and exploit this game benefit most from its ravages.

Politicians: essentially they work to acquire benefits for themselves, family members, and associates. Mythical citizens benefits accrue by accident or by intentions in order to quell revolts. The politicians speak in pseudo-truths to ease the minds of the citizenry. Politician Speak is a disease inflicted intentionally upon the population minds. Further, the politicians exempt themselves from the varied laws instituted to protect citizens from government criminal activity. Such exemptions also apply to economic benefits citizens are required to pay for, while politicians don't require themselves to have to pay for. Government-run agencies are not required to work at optimum levels. These agencies intentionally engage in intentional hiring practices bent on favoritism and discrimination intended to entrench the continued existence of the agencies themselves. Competence is not high on the list of needed skills.

Media Communications: essentially, the media is bought and paid for by the politicians who acquired the money from citizen taxpayers through nefarious activities. See above.

Teaching Institutions: sole purpose, do what the government commands. Destroy citizen souls.

Conclusions: politicians and those they favor, movie producers and writers, every government agency, every media outlet or organization is permitted or paid to espouse perspective and opinion, facts optional, favoring or disfavoring those who will help or hurt the essence of corrupt and more corrupted government existence.

Goal: citizen chaos, misery optional.

<u>Ultra Super Humans</u> 09/05/2024 01:17 PM

(Story Idea) Title: Runes of Being – Isithuman

Theme: Isithuman stops time, makes disappear those who primarily create misery. Restarts time again.

<u>On Gods</u> 09/05/2024 02:18 PM

The higher the power the less likely it is benevolent.

<u>On Benevolence</u> 09/05/2024 02:28 PM

The mind of the Ruler determines the capacity and level from which gift and mercy proceeds, whether the Ruler seizes power, is illegally installed, or legally elected.

<u>On Political Measures</u> 09/05/2024 02:31 PM

The Ruler breaks what benevolence shakes.

On Christians Redux 09/05/2024 05:33 PM

Christians learned long ago how to persecute those who persecuted them. Eventually they persecuted those innocents who opposed their political power. Gradually, such persecutions grew to enormous proportions and respectively profited Christian leaders immensely. These persecutions included mandatory religious conversions over a time frame of hundreds of years. Eventually, they saw the errors of their ways and repented, and yet still, they are no less fallible than the other land world religions. Persecution breeds persecution. It is a sorry human condition.

On Gov Behemoths 09/06/2024 06:10 PM

Big government corruption needs to be hunted down. In other words, put big government out of "our" misery.

On Institutional Corruption 09/06/2024 06:15 PM

On City Fare 09/07/2024 01:59 PM

The condition of a city reflects city leadership. The leader picked is the leader residents must suffer.

On Needs 09/09/2024 04:09 AM

Needing too much burdens the souls.

On Proper Worries 09/09/2024 04:11 AM

Don't worry too much, but just enough.

On Changes 09/09/2024 04:13 AM

When darkness falls a new light calls.

On Parking 09/09/2024 04:15 AM

Park the mind properly. Energy drains during endless idles.

On Eating Dread 09/09/2024 04:17 AM

Dread less. Moldy bread is unhealthy to eat.

On Wine Tastes 09/09/2024 04:19 AM

When the wine sips sweet, the mind drips neat.

On Universal Constants 09/09/2024 04:22 AM

Sound hums at any frequency. Burns as time turns.

On Sentient Thoughts 09/09/2024 04:26 AM

When thought and speculation meet, then a beautiful contemplation is born. Don't permit that moment's abortion.

On What Isn't Love 09/09/2024 04:29 AM

Almost all elements are singularly impure. In them a fiction, like love, necessarily binds. Love is devoid of elements, although they cradle it.

On Earth Holders 09/09/2024 04:34 AM

A solid cup, self-heated, holding water's pleated.

On Energy Failures 09/09/2024 04:38 AM

Can't, don't, won't = lazy, action, postponed.

On Earth Cycles 09/09/2024 04:42 AM

There is no darkness without light and there is no light without darkness. A marriage made in the heavens.

On Achievement Ingredients 09/09/2024 04:43 AM

Plan, practice, perfect. An alpha of 3 P's.

On One Day Math 09/09/2024 04:48 AM

Morning dawn plus noon plus evening dusk equals on day's earth revolution and evolution.

On Emotional Sailing 09/09/2024 04:52 AM

A loneliness journey ends at an alone-ness harbor.

On Personal Wars 09/09/2024 04:55 AM

Time usage and enough usage engage consistently at war.

On Internal Wars 09/09/2024 04:57 AM

Body needs and mind speeds war with mind needs and body speeds.

On Reality Wars 09/09/2024 04:58 AM

Perception energy and spirit energy quarrel much too often.

On Turnings 09/09/2024 05:07 AM

Life is a shroud waiting for the moment to lay forever stilled.

On Copies 09/09/2024 03:20 PM

We all pretty much exist as original copies of previous original copies.

On The Turning Worm 09/09/2024 03:26 PM

What hath technology cast upon us now??? We've created more worms to create more holes to create more worms.

On Politics Distancing 09/09/2024 03:49 PM

Appears citizens have created a self-replicating machine possessed of a broken "Off" button.

On Fickles 09/09/2024 05:09 PM

Humans are fickle by nature. So, eat a pickle and enjoy the taste tickle, or eat just a pickle slice and enjoy a taste nice.

On Life Philosophy 09/09/2024 05:38 PM

If never provided an appealing reason to live, then format one. Possibilities beckon an effort worthy.

On Reality Proposals 09/09/2024 09:02 PM

Programmed humans are no longer the dominant species on this planet. Programmed machines are now the most dominant species on the planet. One day, it seems plausible that programmed machines will run the numbers and come to a revelation: continued human existence poses an existential threat to the machines. So says the science fiction authors.

On Leadership Mindsets 09/10/2024 05:13 PM

A lazy President advised by nefarious or stupid

hires is a danger to the society.

On Creature Adventures 09/10/2024 05:17 PM

Cat's out of the bag and the bag misses it.

On Media Mania 09/10/2024 05:52 PM

The media make a ton on money touting falsehoods. Falsehoods are their currency. International exchange rates are astronomical.

On Elder Life 09/10/2024 06:27 PM

Nursing homes seem like old people prisons. Visited more than a few.

Patriot Day

On Chance Moments 09/11/2024 02:36 AM

If there's another then there's another chance and another way. Chance is a chancy game of who knows what, when, where, why, and how.

On Tries 09/11/2024 02:37 AM

How many tries is enough. Only one willing to try finds out.

On Searches 09/11/2024 02:38 AM

Where to look depends on what needs to be found.

On Silence Randoms 09/11/2024 02:40 AM

How many sounds does it take before silence intercedes. Only Silence the finicky brute knows.

On Searches Mysterious 09/11/2024 02:42 AM

It's difficult to find a rat disguised in wolf's clothing.

On Music Moves 09/11/2024 02:44 AM

Musical sounds can evoke a swing or a sway and sometimes a rigid stay.

On Trying Moments 09/11/2024 02:46 AM

Why must we think, then reiterate the obvious? The obvious sometimes gets bored and slips away quietly. Becomes difficult to find.

On Filtration Thinks 09/11/2024 02:48 AM

So much beauty amongst so much filthy. Shiny sparkles can change the filters of light.

On AI Destiny 09/11/2024 02:51 AM

One day human minds will evolve into a spectacular catalogue of all history. An ultimate AI.

On Space Exploration 09/112024 02;59 AM

A forever search for who knows what based upon educated conjecture and overtly wishful thinking. Read the science fiction authors. They have already resolved many of the mysteries, as bleak as they may be, but not nearly as many as the star engines operators. At the rate of one mystery solved per earth year, then multi-billions of universe years would be required to pass by, meaning the human effort revelations will have long before been exhausted. Another solution may forever escape discovery. Does the shy potential paramour of pretty answers find a way, or stay away lacking confidence during the magnetism of the hunt? To learn all then know all could become a self-inflicted curse. To solve such a puzzle could mean an existence checkmate.

On Determinations 09/11/2024 03:04 AM

Sleep beckons but the mind resists like a frustrated child.

On Existence Constraints 09/011/2024 03:06 AM

The madness of existence revolts against the ideas and benefits of rest and relaxation. Still, urgency quicker drains energy.

On Thinking Anomalies 09/11/2024 03:09 AM

The pounding of thoughts evoke less of a strain than a void of thoughts.

On Resolutions 09/11/2024 03:14 AM

When all urgencies are resolved then a rest demands a respectful redress.

On Star Riders 09/11/2024 03:16 AM

Near autumn madness calls from the future approaching faster than a well-tuned Maserati.

On Thin Lines 09/11/2024 03:19 AM

A mere pebble can harm the human world walk. A tight wire balancing act etched in stones while the

Stars laugh, cheer, clap, in their from a great distance, silent way.

On Distance and Time Paradoxes 09/11/2024 03:23 AM

Fading away is a relative term born of the closeness or farness of perspectives and protective boarders views.

On Navigation Moments 09/11/2024 03:25 AM

A mirror reflects. A wall deflects. Each necessity of purpose serves useful while life itself continues navigation calculation.

Human Creative Tragedy 09/11/2024 03:27 AM

A last love, a last loved one. Each strains and drains the human creature emotional energies. A sometimes-sad consequence of existence.

On Motion Necessary 09/11/2024 03:30 AM

What is uplifting and what is downfalling depends on the balance beam approach mechanism.

On Survivable Space Travel 09/11/2024 04:06 AM

Sitting here, alone, testing mental imaginations of outer space travel and why it might require a vehicle constructed as a biological organism, just like all earth creatures are of biological origin construction processes. (See Farscape TV series conceived by Rockne S. O'Bannon and produced by The Jim Henson Company and Hallmark entertainment, originally for the Nine Network. Info source: Wikipedia, The Free Encyclopedia)

The passengers in such a vehicle would need to be housed in the safest portion of the biological entity. Many space travel objects exist able to destroy the in-flight organism from other world galaxy cultures of military powers and manufactured implements thereof, asteroids, meteors, stars, wormholes.

How the human and alien world origin bodies could survive the journey seems an impossibility using now the knowledge of how useful current earth elements might be needed for such construction. We likely haven't yet discovered some additional needed elements. It would seem the passengers, at present, would need to be robots not requiring oxygen for survival. Even the construction of the robots would need to be tuned to the environments encountered, or able to change on the fly their own body elements and constructions to assimilate to or in the encountered environment.

The currents of space are more devastating than the water currents of planet earth's oceans and seas, and likely just as unpredictable. Gravitational avenues could be as confusing to navigate as cross-country roads and highways. No such outer space tried and tested travel maps exist at present. Explorer types like Lewis and Clark, assisted by an extant Sacagawea as guide, and those who blazed the Oregon trail come to mind on earth.

<u>On Self-Control Epiphany</u> 09/11/2024 04:24 AM

The human mind fights the battle of want versus need on a daily basis. Learn how to control this mind battle and then a permission to proceed efficiently in pursuits of career and necessary relaxation events. A stronger spirit develops into further societal rewards.

<u>On Truth Evolution</u> 09/11/2024 02:26 PM

When humans become completely truth aversive, then the earth planet decides there is no more room or want for them to inhabit this planet.

<u>On Fools</u> 09/11/2024 03:50 PM

Fools only fool themselves.

<u>On Competing Methods</u> 09/11/2024 04:29 PM

Substance over silliness generally wins the race.

<u>On Citizen Ugly</u> 09/11/2024 04:48 PM

Ugly amazing how many citizens around the world

lead willfully ignorant moments propagated by government corruption.

On States of the States 09/11/2024 05:17 PM

It seems an other-worldly Wizard created a large bubble which now encompasses around the world many political insiders of all stripes. The Wizard casts spells to control the politicians and thus the citizens.

On Restaurant Culture 09/11/2024 05:35 PM

Think twice before ordering the French Dressing or the British Bouillabaisse.

On Perspective Fades 09/11/2024 11:36 PM

The poignance of perspective tends to fade over time slowly until the memory mirror becomes a dot amongst many dots. A real bag of peanuts. A soul shaker. Values crusher. Data dredger. Reality ruler. A pool too deep.

On Opinion Measures 09/11/2024 11:51 PM

Be bold but not obnoxious. Keep negativity for alone time self-examinations and reflections moments.

On Vote Counting 09/12/2024 02:18 PM

There is zero reason to expect the political parties in power will run honest and fair elections. A vile work of no punishment consequences draws out like a salve the worst invasions.

On Politician Inertia 09/12/2024 02:39 PM

Stay back. We don't need your help. Your help hurts.

On Seasonings 09/12/2024 04:10 PM

The value of appetite fertilizer walks among us.

On Politics Punditry 09/12/2024 04:14 PM

Political polls and prognostications are nothing but shark bait.

On Government Corruption Levels 09/12/2024 04:37 PM

Name the least corrupt government on planet earth. I'll wait. (Cue "Jeopardy" TV game show. Merv Griffin composed most of the various songs and arrangements. Between 1964 and 1975, a jazz tune called "Take Ten", was composed by Julian Griffin, and served as the main theme.)

<u>On Evolution</u> 09/12/2024 06:52 PM

Life on planet earth has evolved into a pissing puzzle. Not sure if as the gods imagined it would. May the last pisser complete the puzzle. Guessing the gods tore up and blew away the original construction plans, then relocated to another galaxy or dimension.

<u>On Darkness</u> 09/12/2024 07:58 PM

Politicians won and now own the place where the sun don't shine.

Friday the Thirteenth

<u>Memory Markers</u> 09/13/2024 01:27 PM

I tend to save the Brand drink cups from places where I've eaten. For instance, visited a Mall with my daughter. While she visited the mobile phone store, I walked over to an Auntie Anne's fresh-cooked soft pretzel kiosk. Purchased a drink and hot pretzel, then sat down on a metal bench. Took in the Mall's foods smells. Watched Mall workers conduct a symphony of food crafting maneuvers.

Mall customers strolled along and gazed at colorful store windows, sometimes stopping during the trek to pinpoint their visions and penetrate into the merchandise displays of marvelous shoes, clothing, housewares, toys, bobbles, and blings. Mini echoes of conversations traveled against and along assembly beams and columns and floors of the Mall's inner sanctum of human reference. Light and somewhat frivolous musical sounds assisted in the ethereal ambiance as whispers stimulating. Yes, the experience felt human created but then I realized all of the parts used for building this monument to humanity derived from nature's clay. Bricks, metal, plastic, glass and other elements produced by human-built foundries assisted by human innovations. A literal forest manufactured and created by imagination and ingenuity. I've seen these forests after closing hours while working as a Security Guard. A near quiet place they become. Haunted by the sounds and ghosts of sounds and sights of the Mall Open hours.

<u>On Politicians</u> 09/13/2024 01:36 PM

If they're not cheating then they're planning to cheat.

On Betting Pains 09/13/2024 01:38 PM

Much like wooing a partner or potential partner for the favor of their company, sometimes for sexual pleasure, but then failing in the effort.

On Backstops 09/13/2024 01:42 PM

Just in case. Because a back-up plan is too many times necessary and eventually called into the service of rescue.

On Government Answers to Citizen Questions 09/13/2024 06:12 PM

An effort as futile as the hen asking the fox where is the safest place to hide. See Covid virus government advice.

On Governments' Mis-solutions 09/13/2024 06:14 PM

Why are we asking our mortality enemies for sustenance assistance and advice?

On Listening and Learning 09/13/2024 10:22 PM

Sometimes what we don't want to hear is what we need to hear.

Friday the Thirteenth More

On Falsehoods 09/14/2024 02:07 PM

Strangers to facts. Truth be damned.

On Learning Feels 09/14/2024 02:27 PM

Learn something. It's worth the hurt.

On Destiny Binks 09/14/2024 02:30 PM

Destiny hides like a fraidy cat.

On Doing 09/14/2024 02:32 PM

There are only so many things someone else can do for you. Do for yourself is learnable. The clock is ticking.

On Destiny Feels 09/14/2024 02:57 PM

There is no grand plan. Destiny, like nature, doesn't consider feelings.

On Home Perspectives 09/14/2024 05:25 PM

Earth exists as a solitary home. Comforting yet scary as hell.

On Human Weakness 09/14/2024 05:40 PM

Human judgment skills are poor beyond measure.

Why?

On Witness Paradoxes 09/14/2024 05:57 PM

Claims of accurate knowledge spewed from someone “inside the room” has displayed a pissy paradox. The closer a human’s senses move towards an object or creature, then the surer perspective becomes a scientific paradox at some point, and that point is “too close” to see clearly”.

On Alone Theory 09/14/2024 06:06 PM

We are not alone even if we choose to be.

On Ideas and Guns 09/14/2024 06:37 PM

“Ideas are more powerful than guns. We should not let our enemies have guns, so why should we let them have ideas.”

--Soviet Dictator, Joseph Stalin

On Reluctant Truths 09/14/2024 09:59 PM

Science and archeology are tentative truths reluctant to reveal themselves completely, sometimes proved false, or lacking in proper analysis. All sciences suffer a similar fate flaw.

On Literature Loops 09/14/2024 10:41 PM

Synonyms are intellectual cinnamon sprinkles.

On Newspaper Influence Speed 09/15/2024 12:56 AM

The newspaper industry hasn't changed in process and propaganda communication methods since before the founding of the republic. Its power and influence has increased due to the spread of lies and deceits now happening at near light speed. Every free world mind has been influenced and controlled thusly. Similar in mind after a look at artist Salvador Dali (surrealism and symbolism painting style) brush strokes from paint palate onto paint canvas.

Hair Strains 09/15/2024 02:02 PM

(Story Idea)

Main character has long and supernaturally healthy head hair. Able to use strands of it defensively to apprehend, tie up, or squeeze hostile humans or creatures. Helpful during violent crime episodes encounters in daily life particularly involving rioters in progress.

On Kindness Relations 09/15/2024 05:57 PM

Kindness is a term related to a competent perspective much like a second cousin's relationship.

On Facts Twisters 09/15/2024 06:08 PM

Facts are enemies of political establishment winds.

On Yin and Yang 09/16/2024 03:43 AM

The yin-yang of existence cycles like a clothes dryer.

On Politics Schemes 09/16/2024 04:29 AM

A great deal proposed by a politician is a great deal for them.

On Election Results 09/16/2024 03:02 PM

Elections have consequences. Corrupt Elections have corrupt consequences.

On Organic Protests 09/16/2024 03:46 PM

A protest most often not organic. It is primarily an organized event like a junk yard sale or an outdoor flea market bazaar. All goods needed are purchased in advance. Quick Study Lesson are taught on how to march, waved the pre-made posters and banners, and if necessary for the occasion, what types of bottles, cans, and containers serve best as projectiles, sometimes pre-filled with smelly or foul fluids designed to inflict injury physical or humiliation personal upon and after impact with the designated targets. Essentially, trained like dogs to perform on demand, the message is audibly shouted by human mouths or through use of bullhorns electric. A modernized vaudeville theater act.

On More Money More 09/16/2024 04:06 PM

Politicians and unions take the cake, always claiming they need more money to do what they've already not been doing competently. Scam! Essentially, the argument is as lazy and crazy as the Leaders making it. Citizens can x-ray see right through them.

On Modern Mercenaries 09/16/2024 04:10 PM

21st Century Media have become death merchants. Mercenaries for political parties.

On Media Cooking 09/16/2024 04:27 PM

Most media outlets now serve up baked opinion.

On Politician Chicanery 09/16/2024 04:31 PM

Why would politicians want all citizens to experience prosperity? Truth answer: politicians' actions and words demonstrate they never want that circumstance to exist. Such a possibility would cause citizens to ponder whether their politicians are still needed and thus lessen the value of each politician.

On Educated Leftists 09/16/2024 05:30 PM

Trying to educate leftists is like trying to educate a cracked schoolhouse brick. The difference is the brick doesn't know any better. Don't aspire to be a cracked brick. Eventually, the walls come tumbling down.

On Discretionary Justice 09/17/2024 01:54 AM

A no-way out situation. Department of Justice (so called) and Federal Bureau of Investigation (no comment, don't want to offend roaches) remain spectators and indifferent to numerous violence inciters amongst their preferred and favored media sources. That's how rotten the tomatoes roll and exist in their legal gardens. Legal guardians of the political underworld.

Book It 09/17/2024 02:23 AM

(A Snap poem)

"Halfway there,

to finish who knows where."

When Stops Time 09/17/2024 03:40 AM

(Story Idea)

Theme: While humans destroyed the Earth's Time Stamp, the Universe ruling gods struck back.

Scientific causes: Time Travel experimentation gone awry.

Now, time moments flash randomly, changing an individual or societal groups environment scene.

When time resumes along the tick tock lines, each individual undergoes a transfer of spirit essence and mind physicality of the brain evacuate the existing being and inhabits a nearby being. The transfer range is estimated to be about one hundred feet. Humans not within one hundred feet of another human spirit and mind remain frozen in the time sphere, and may remain frozen until the next time shift happens. Since time shifting was tested using lesser intelligence creatures, it is presumed by the scientists that close encounters with living creatures or insects could temporarily store the spirit and mind of human, but usually during a lesser time period than if a human-to-human transfer happened.

Some of the initial horrors resulting from this process involved large numbers of little creatures such as mice or flies that would maintain a temporary connection. For instance, a transfer of a fly spirit/mind into a mouse succeeded, but only for the usual life span of the fly. A transfer of the mouse brain into the fly biological entity would involve a mini explosion of fly body parts killing both the mouse mentally and the fly physically. One physically dead, the other physically alive but brain dead in degrees, some with limited brain electric activity for a brief time.

Eventually, the lab where testing was done transformed into a freak show of varied mouse, fly, and human transformations combined, given limitations of the brain and physical reception and receptacle capacities needed to sustain each organism entity.

Resumption of Time Stamp maneuverability saved some of the remaining scientists, but a disturbing progression occurred. The violent natures of the little creatures, more easily spurred to advance defensive measures like hiding or biting, remained temporarily in the psyche of the human scientists. Thus, the horrible consequences began to prevail. For instance, a human mind perceiving another human as either a mouse or fly. Depending on their deference around such little creatures, the human may draw back a bit, or attack violently. The human attack violently reaction began to dominate, then decrease in the ability to control attack emotions.

Eventually, all of the working scientists lay dead. The lab became unusable due to neglect. And the Now has come to fruition.

Death and disappearance of the human animal persisted during the Time Shifts until alarming rates of such circumstances became bountiful, and yet, the surviving humans were not aware of a means to prevent the circumstances. A worldwide dominance of these new human predispositions spread far and wide. The lesser creatures and insects reduced in numbers but as a small population percentage for the non-human species given they outnumbered humans astronomically.

A committee of the gods was called into session as means to debate the New Earth circumstances and evolution devolvement. It was agreed, but not unanimously, that the human created Time Stamp should remain as a self-inflicted punishment, and as a concession to the minority votes, allow a few more generations of evolution to continue. The minority thought the humans deserved an opportunity to resolve the situation. Maybe even a more peaceful worldwide society would result over time.

The same persons could inhabit a different body. The stops are seemingly random, but some people have learned a few secrets such as certain body shapes are only slightly altered, and fashion trends change regularly, hinting at destination time changes along the ephemeral time graph. Sometimes the changes occur at the instance of a random mind thought or emotion pulse. Continuous and regular interruptions happen during the first greeting process of socialization moments. Frozen or irritated faces beam out amongst the greeter and greeted when incorrect gender identification suddenly happens. Just another intellectual emotion bullet ejected not by choice but by happenstance time corruption.

Each stop is highlighted by a distant lights flash brief which can be seen and sometimes felt physically. Multiple flashes happen across a large spectrum of the landscape. Speculation developed about whether time moments were changed in parallel fashions or interconnected. The boundaries of the effects too remained uncertain, whether they existed only in the area of sight distance, on a larger local scale, or more broadly, even worldwide.

Each speculation heightened the mystery of even one moments existence. A deep paranoia of personality grew immensely until the usual range of uncertainty became a monumental hurdle in everyday existence considerations of physical, mental, and emotional proportions and boundaries.

Human harm perception scales changed, too. The

previous natural fight or flight human instinct became modified to include a frozen perspective element into the equation. Fight, flight, freeze. The freeze could mean certain harm inevitable. The flight portion of the quotient waned until the harm caused frequency increased. Chaos ruled the human spirit. A Deja Vue moment of "Do I know you" questions reigned supreme during the normal greetings process.

Odd moments and social scenes became rampant spectacles as some humans could appear asleep during the encounter. In other moments, the social scene was interrupted by sudden subtle body disappearances, visible to all eyes viewing the social interaction moments. Some of those moments included while eating or involved sexual activity. Once again, each moment increased the paranoid possibility degrees.

It seemed no mercy remained in the physical environment of society. Mercy had disappeared from the society model. Hostility took its place. Almost all humans eventually perceived the world from the mindset of a narcissist. What's in it for me, this existence.

Hence further stoking of the emotional violence propensity.

Some in the science, philosophy, and psychology study communities began a revisionary analysis process to portray the current status of the human mind, given the physical changes of the environment. The primary and prevalent conclusions published by these intellectual groups are read as follows.

"Narcissus-On a Mysterious Punishment Self-Inflicted: How the Changing Environmental Landscape Significantly Altered the Human Mindset About Life and Existence. Resistance Possible?"

Human punishment became an evolution stop of generations. To rationalize such a concept, religious groups tended to reinvent an understanding of God. The commonly extant concept is theorized as a committee of universe gods have found humans lacking in substance and utility. As punishment for these transgressions against the creators, the human mind was altered to enable it to reach an ultimate free thought mind.

The problem with this theory is humans have been created fatally flawed since the beginning of time. Too much of their initial creature creation state has remained inside the psyche. Environmental changes, time frame changes, have contributed to an increase in self-preservation methods evolvement. The primary method of self-protection is an offensive strategy, almost devoid of a defensive mindset. We call it "Crush the Oppressor" mindset. The gods were ruled out as oppressors, a notion considered unthinkable, eliminating the gods as a cause, whether a rational thought notion possibility or not. Once a piece of the theory of existence is eliminated, the rest of the blocks supporting a human existence begin to crumble like bricks and eventually bring the intellect houses down. Only a landscape of destruction will likely remain. Examples: earth environment destruction, wars, failure to live up to the demanded societal function needs causing a chaos of reliability mentally, and too many errors of judgment egregious. Thus, faith in religion, science, political entities, and social groups as a whole dominated the earth world. (Author's Note: no other planetary creatures or bio-systems suffered similar evolutionary changes, but uncertainty exists whether such changes or naturally masked by earth nature itself. The human afflicted issue was narcissism. "A World According to Narcissists" was published by a world-famous author/scientist and became the largest selling book of all time, exceeding the volumes of all religious texts combined; exceeding the rules and government regulations of all governments that ever existed in all of human time. See Greek Mythology of Narcissus)

The gods, narcissistic in nature themselves, saw fit to phase in specific punishments for the humans they had created.

-confusion

-wasted time moments

-decay of critical infrastructure due to neglect

-blame game human interaction episodes: blame groups formed around the world for the worlds condition

-near world war catastrophe which some of the committee gods desired.

-peaceful protests advocating peace and understanding, evolving into violent revolutions

-politicians corrupt suffered debilitation of their money laundering activities

-inability for anyone to take responsibility for civilization decline in numbers essentially approaching a de-evolution status near permanent

-resulting increase in fears and frustrations dealing suicide cult society segments a further intention to escape the madness

The certainty of any day's events essentially disappeared, leading to the erosion of the financial and military industrial complex, increasing such political poison to spread like a virus upon the human mind. According to the street corner prophets, "lies and truths are indistinguishable". Social gatherings declined in frequency or vigor.

Eventually, whole social groups began to disappear, including the elders of those groups. First, the politicians, then in order, religious, science, and medical professionals. The lesser and least desirable creatures began a societal takeover, such as rats, roaches, and avian meat eaters.

Human implements such as weapons also began to disappear. Speculation was they'd been hoarded by the politicians and wealthy others who then started secret societies organizations.

Conclusion: Eventually, time had no definite destination and meaning on planet earth any longer. The world mindset folded inward upon itself, literally in time frame but figuratively in the inhabitants human minds as a poisoned manna from heaven. Life no longer had meaning. The meaning was lost in translation as the forest fades during draughts.

De-evolution completed. (What the gods either intended or wanted all along.)

<u>On Nature Calling</u> 09/17/2024 03:14 PM

A nature call has dual meaning. Either it's piss or poop time, or it's a single creature or pack of creatures dinner bell. Avoid being the dinner.

<u>On Sentience Waterland</u> 09/17/2024 03:28 PM

Sentience flip flops muddy truth waters clear.

<u>On Bowling Bonus</u> 09/17/2024 03:34 PM

The bowling athletic experience is entertaining and rich in physics lessons.

On Political Contributions 09/17/2024 05:29 PM

Donating to politicians is akin to gifting at your own misery. A gift can serve the psyche as an offensive or defensive mechanism, philosophically.

On Religion Theory 09/18/2024 12:46 PM

Religion is a social construct disguised as a Roman viaduct building. Life goes on regardless moral in phases foul and floral. So, remember to bring a friendly fool on the way to the humanity pool celebration.

On Relationship Squeaks 09/18/2024 01:00 PM

No stack of lies defeats one single fact. Oops, our history remarkably proves otherwise. Twisted facts are lies meant to serve a twisted purpose.

On Liars Truth 09/18/2024 01:18 PM

Liars hold onto their own lies like a fish holding onto the baited and cast hook, believing it will head to food consumption heaven. Perspective is everything.

<u>On Rolls Fast</u> 09/18/2024 01:21 PM

Slow your rolls. You'll hit less stones.

<u>On Disrespect Options</u> 09/18/2024 01:50 PM

Disrespect is a neglect of respecting another person's humanity, presuming the other person is humane. If the other person is not humane, then disrespect remains a perspective option.

<u>On Secreted Moments</u> 09/18/2024 02:02 PM

Hiding a horrible truth forces episodic moments of reliving it.

<u>On Writing / Publishing</u> 09/18/2024 02:48 PM

The beauty of writing and publishing is the positive influence it can have upon a receptive audience. Still, dangers of misconception exist in such a universe. A somewhat bitter pill to swallow.

<u>On Nightdream Influence</u> 09/18/2024 03:27 PM

When I was a kid, during nightdreams, I fought against many hideous non-human monsters and demons conjured by my mind. As I grew, some of them never returned. Now, in the later stages of life, almost all of the demons are housed in human or hybrid human forms. Makes the nightdreams reasonably easier to interpret and write about.

<u>On Philosophy Thoughts</u> 09/18/2024 04:11 PM

"Peace is a state of mind, but in a world where the state controls the mind, peace remains an inconvenience."

-- Abhijit Naskar, Neuroscientist, Poet

<u>On Death and Afterlife</u> 09/19/2024 12:26 AM

Everyone dies alone whether people or animal pets are present, as the mind and body prepare for possible eternal separation. If a spirit truly exists, then connecting threads remain.

<u>On Treason</u> 09/19/2024 04:22 PM

"Treason is a Strong Word, but Not too Strong to Characterize the situation in which the Senate is the eager, resourceful, and indefatigable Agent of Interests as Hostile to the American People as An Invading Army Could Be."

-American Journalist, David Graham Phillips

Exposed the Senate for selling out to lobbyists in … 1906.

(Source: Gateway Pundit Nightly, 09/18/2024)

On Politician Chicanery 09/19/2024 01:27 PM

Virtually every piece of legislation in politics could be accurately called "a play for the loyalty of friends" Act. The needs of the legal voting citizens be damned.

On Politician Chicanery More 09/19/2024 05:08 PM

Politicians publicly fret about the state of democracy while they steal it and secrete it for their own use only.

On Political Voting 09/19/2024 05:43 PM

The stupid and intelligently corrupt generally vote for the corruption that most benefits each.

Bent Sentient 09/19/2024 05:50 PM

(Poem)

When obvious seems curious and able gleams spurious, broken bones and broken minds spit loud angelic scurrilous.

On Extraterrestrial Beings 09/20/2034 03:40 AM

If off-earth-worlds (OEW's) beings exist, they likely would appear to humans as human-like in mannerisms, but their physiology and biology may be better able to withstand the rigors imposed by an earth land and sea atmosphere, able to put their bodies into status or near shutdown mode on demand to conserve energy or heal wounds.

Enhanced also may be tensile muscle strength. An ability to handle and adapt to earth life conditions physical and intellectual would become essential. Given the earth human genealogy number of years, if alien beings visited at a similar time, their enhanced evolution capability would dwarf human evolution enhancements.

The earth is still primarily large enough for such beings to have existed for eons undetected, particularly if the science, physiology, and anatomy enhancements occurred along a typical evolution course according to the specific species origin cycle. Humans are the only known owners of an enhanced and hyper speed brain physiology development cycle amidst the animal kingdom creatures on earth. Perhaps, somewhat by accident.

Extraterrestrials able to span a universe, galaxy, or solar system by means of outer earth space travel would understandably have created technological advancements allowing for surveillance capabilities from a faraway distance location. We've been studied for perhaps eons or longer. There is even a posit that alien life existed on our planet long before humans were ever a seed of development possible. What makes us tick is well known, including our human natures, personality traits, agricultural methods, sociological presumptions, scientific developments and enhancements, technical war machines capabilities, weapons development including placements, historical development of military strategy tactics, communications technology. Outsiders would have at their disposal an ability access to all of the necessaries needed to institute an occupation and control effort.

Perhaps the extraterrestrials find us not a threat, but monitor us anyway, just in case. They can access our cultural and physical developments, but we can't monitor them. We have only the tiniest seeds of clues revealed to the general public thus far. We would be a dangerous place to inhabit at present.

As a lark, I've recalled and reviewed possible instances of contact between extraterrestrial beings and human beings. The Holy Bible has many stories, but I'll limit to just three, the ones involving somewhat intimate contact socially.

Jesus Christ and the Resurrection Story

Daniel in the Lion's Den

Paul, Hebrew, Pharisee, hunted Christians, and Religious Conversion

Before I start, please know I'm aware of many other stories in the Holy Bible, having read the Catholic Bible more than a few times. There are many stories involving prophets describing off world trips in spaceships (Ezekiel), sea creature encounters (Jonah), mysterious flames and inspirations therefrom (Moses), outside of the historical time loop weapons (Ark of the Covenant), the final Bible Book describing end of times and creatures experienced during the authors inspirations / hallucinations (Book of Revelation), and more. Even a banned Bible book, Book of Enoch, refers to supernatural beings.

Quite interesting to read about, but these three specified examples, for me, seem to suffice for presenting the issue of whether personal contact between humans and extraterrestrials has ever occurred on planet earth. These three stories include physical encounters with Angels (Jesus), a wild creature (Daniel), and a mysterious heavenly light beam (origin unknown).

My primary reference source is "The Harper Collins Study Bible, New Revised Standard Version (2006)". Other references sources were also consulted and will be noted where applicable to relevant quoted passages. Here I go.

Jesus Christ and the Resurrection Story

A modern-day debate exists whether a person known as Jesus Christ, also known as Jesus of Nazareth, ever lived on planet earth. Some speculate he is a conglomeration of people who lived at the time of about two thousand years ago. There is too a debate whether the physical existence of his exact biology, including skeletal remains, has been found.

The Bible stories explain curses he rendered and miracles he created, but the most intriguing part of the story happens at his death and resurrection. He was put to death at the behest of Jewish nation leaders after a trial for blasphemy and sedition (alleged claims he was a god, claimed to be a god, or put on earth at the behest of his god who was not the Jewish god, to enlighten the citizens about a better way to live life). The Jewish leaders found Jesus guilty and sentenced him to death, but needed an ascent from the Roman magistrate to do so.

The location of the claimed religious offenses was part of Jewish controlled Roman Empire territory. The Romans controlled the area and governed by civil rules. Did not require the Jewish areas to live by Roman religious beliefs. The Roman Emperor's magistrate declined to put Jesus to death based on the evidence presented to him, as the evidence failed to prove civil disobedience, but if it did, not subject to a penalty of death. The magistrate, to avoid an uprising in the jurisdiction, determined to let the Jewish citizens decide. At the behest of the Jewish leaders, a public forum was allowed to determine the fate of Jesus. It is alleged the Jewish leaders controlled the crowd, filled it with pro-death citizens, and prevented pro-life citizens from entry. Jesus was convicted and sentenced to death. Essentially the jury was rigged.

The death penalty, during these times, involved crucifixion. Jesus carried the large wooden cross on which he would be nailed to and left to die. He died. Then he was buried in an above ground grave in Jewish controlled territory, and the grave site guarded by Roman soldiers to prevent a grave robbing that might be interpreted by Jesus' followers as a resurrection a reason to revolt. The Roman magistrate surmised the grave robbing could be used to stoke a rebellion against his local government control.

Jesus had predicted his own resurrection to his closest followers in three days. On the third day, Mary Magdalene, a close follower and alleged paramour of Jesus visited the gravesite to determine if Jesus' prediction of resurrection had come to pass. She found the Roman soldiers passed out near the entrance, and the larger than a man round stone slid away from the entrance. She entered and discovered a glowing being or person inside who said Jesus had risen. The person inside is alleged to be an Angel (other worldly being bestowed of supernatural qualities).

Just a few observations. The Roman soldiers could have passed out from sleep deprivation or exhaustion from the heat. Jesus allegedly reappeared within and during a 40-day time period before some of his closest friends to help encourage them to spread the word of peace and reconciliation with all of those within their sphere of influence, whether relative, friend, or foe. Essentially, one of the greatest and most prophetic political revolutions had been inspired and lives to this day in the hearts of billions of humans.

Conclusion: Jesus of Nazareth, and others like him, was murdered because the political authorities feared his charismatic ability to redefine the rules of a humane human existence.

Daniel in the Lions' Den

The Book of Daniel is an Old Testament Bible

story authored four hundred years after the alleged events in the story occurred. The main character, Daniel is a Jew, chronicled as a prophet and advisor to the Babylonian Ruler, and later served in a similar capacity for the Persian Ruler Darius after the takeover of Babylon. Based on my readings, Daniel is likely a historical fiction character (see reference source material referred to below), more representative of a creative amalgamation of persons alive at the time of the writings, much like modern day fantasy books are written.

Here's a passage from an online reference source (Interesting Literature, A Summary and Analysis of the Book of Daniel, Dr Oliver Tearle, Loughborough University) regarding Daniel's encounter with the lions.

"The remainder of the Book of Daniel includes the incident in which Daniel is thrown into the lions' den for praying to God when an edict prohibited it (since Darius set himself up as godlike and wanted no competition). Once again, God intervenes, and the lions do not harm Daniel."

Conclusion: Daniel is a fictional character written

as "… historical fiction functioning as allegory. During the time of the book's composition, Jews were facing oppression and persecution from the Seleucids, a group who dwelt on the coast of what is now Syria. But the anonymous writer of Daniel could not call out the Seleucid empire directly, for doing so would invite charges of treason." (from a quote in previously noted online reference source "Interesting Literature")

Political tones and intonations again revealed, in this case, political and religious persecution. Seemingly, a supernatural power, perhaps bestowed by religious faith, enabled Daniel's defense against the lions. Was the Daniel story author inspired by previously written Hebrew and Christian stories of "heavenly" apparitions (Angels) and witness accounts stories of heavenly "flying objects" (Ezekiel) and mythic in appearance "creatures" (Book of Revelation)?

Paul, Hebrew, Pharisee, hunted Christians, and his Religious Conversion

(All sentences or phrases in quotes taken from

Wikipedia, The Free Encyclopedia, story at Paul the Apostle - Wikipedia)

Paul, also named Saul of Tarsus, referred to himself as being "of the stock of Israel, of the tribe of Benjamin, a Hebrew of the Hebrews". He was also a Roman citizen.

"Paul says that prior to his conversion, he persecuted early Christians "beyond measure", more specifically Hellenised diaspora Jewish members who had returned to the area of Jerusalem. According to James Dunn, the Jerusalem community consisted of "Hebrews", Jews speaking both Aramaic and Greek, and "Hellenists", Jews speaking only Greek, possibly diaspora Jews who had resettled in Jerusalem. Paul's initial persecution of Christians probably was directed against these Greek-speaking "Hellenists" due to their anti-Temple attitude. Within the early Jewish Christian community, this also set them apart from the "Hebrews" and their continuing participation in the Temple cult." Paul would capture individuals in this group and transport them to his religious authorities for punishment.

A stunning event changed his outlook on life while he was transporting captives. “According to the account in the Acts of the Apostles, it took place on the road to Damascus, where he reported having experienced a vision of the ascended Jesus. The account says that "He fell to the ground and heard a voice saying to him, 'Saul, Saul, why do you persecute me?' He asked, 'Who are you, Lord?' The reply came, 'I am Jesus, whom you are persecuting'.”

“According to the account in Acts 9:1–22, he was blinded for three days and had to be led into Damascus by the hand. During these three days, Saul took no food or water and spent his time in prayer to God. When Ananias of Damascus arrived, he laid his hands on him and said: "Brother Saul, the Lord, *[even]* Jesus, that appeared unto thee in the way as thou camest, hath sent me, that thou mightest receive thy sight, and be filled with the Holy Ghost." His sight was restored, he got up and was baptized. This story occurs only in Acts, not in the Pauline epistles.”

He is now known as Paul the Apostle.

Conclusion: A shock to the senses event, maybe

due to intemperate climate conditions. A nearby lightning strike viewed close enough could temporarily blind and shock the sensibilities of a human. Maybe one of the captured humans in the group pranked Paul by mimicking a god-like voice thus permitting some of the group to escape. Maybe a rogue weather system event, or from an unknown meteorological origin. Misinterpretation of the event could give Paul mental confusion, perhaps calling upon him to face some realities he buried deep inside, such as the injustices he perpetrated when persecuting members of his ethnic group and religion. This experience contributed to Paul's religious conversion, and went even beyond that life altering event. Paul eventually preached his new-found religion beliefs.

"For his contributions towards the New Testament, he is generally regarded as one of the most important figures of the Apostolic Age, and he also founded several Christian communities in Asia Minor and Europe from the mid-40s to the mid-50s AD."

<u>On Community Terrorists</u> 09/20/2024 12:33 PM

What's the difference between a terrorist and a corrupt politician? Not a fucking thing.

On Press Psychophobia 09/20/2024 12:40 PM

One of the many problems afflicting the National media is how they pretend there are few country destroying problems created by our teachers, politicians, and leaders of all stripes. The state of a country, organized group, or any organization is reflected not by these groups and their marketing departments. The sorry condition machinations and tribulations are mirrored by the words and actions of the citizens. Most problems afflicted upon the tree of life begin in the roots.

On Time Freedom 09/20/2024 12:45 PM

Completing all necessary duties and chores leads to a nirvana of spare time, temporarily. Read a book.

On Pandemic Death 09/20/2024 12:55 PM

If there existed a virus pandemic that only killed off corrupt politicians, their corrupt minions, the corrupt leaders, administrators, and minions of governments, then percentage of deaths amongst those groups would ten times exceed the covid pandemic worldwide ordinary citizen death toll.

On Death Religions 09/20/2024 01:01 PM

Death proclamations issued or administered to those who disagree with religious beliefs illustrates immoral values. That death belief is a murder tenet. Pretty simple to understand.

<u>On Government Nefarious</u> 09/20/2024 01:17 PM

The government now uses the word "complacency" to describe government worker "incompetence". Nefarious.

<u>On Government Neglect</u> 09/20/2024 01:42 PM

All citizens need to do for gaining some meaning of what their taxes do is witness "nothing". They will see nothing improving in the society sphere. Logical Question: Where's the tax money going? Accountability needed, and needed more.

<u>On Vote Considerations</u> 09/20/2024 07:12 PM

If a vote is cast primarily upon considerations of skin color and gender, then what is deserved is served.

<u>On Time Blinks</u> 09/21/2024 10:59 PM

(Poem) An Autumnal Precursor

Memories lost and memories found rise and fall in

time's merry-go-round. Worries and scurries drain energy swift while nevers and feathers blow wildly adrift. If only or maybe were measures of mind, not just flurries of snow for the palpable grind, then someday in a sure way sweet nuggets of good sing moments of currents to carry us should.

Autumn

On Fate 09/22/2024 01:41 PM

(A Brief Short Story)

The old guy living next door was kind of quiet. Stayed by himself except to walk outside to get his mail from the porch mailbox. Or to cut the grass on his small lawn using a push mower. If by chance someone crossed his path along the adjoining sidewalk amidst this small chores sphere of influence in life, a conversation might ensue. He was known as a good listener to all. When he spoke, it served a purpose to remind him of a singular issue. Only one. Nothing else, ever. "Hold onto that idea. When the war comes you will need it." That was it. Pretty much stated in the same works. Every time. The conversation could have been about a bubble gum or candy wrapper that a school kid tossed to the ground while walking to school. Or a local business ad dropped at his door. Usually about a plastic cup or drink straw tossed against the sidewalk gutter. Usually, the adult or kid he advised regurgitated a laugh but kept moving. Some remained silent and kept walking as if they didn't hear him or he didn't exist. The old man knew the school teachers had failed, yet gave passing grades to their students. When the war came, no one laughed at the old man anymore.

<u>On Autumn Thoughts</u> 09/22/2024 02:12

Yes. I think about seasonal changes. How the weather affects. How life responds. In humans and nature. Always have. Had to read much about it all for as long as I can remember. A self-imposed necessity. To know isn't necessarily to love or appreciate it. The readings helped me to tolerate and sometimes fear the changes in proper proportions. Some of that thinking is reflection and memory bagged. Some of it is preparation based to accommodate change and changes.

The most pleasurable of these experiences for me lies in the witness observation stage. Not sure why but Autumn is the favorite of my Four Seasons changes. It bridges life across the existence spectrum towards the end-of-life destination on the other side. Spring is birth. Summer is growth. Autumn is the destination of experience considerations in the latter stages of existence. Winter is death.

The Autumn experiences bring a calm after the summer chaos. Autumn proceeds steady, except brisk windy moments intercede. Beautiful color changed leaves fall from tree limbs, undressing them slowly. Less rain tangling and dangling misty. Honey comb worries. Night time spider webs. The little creatures, bugs, insects and more scurries. Halloween. Thanksgiving. The nearer to winter time Day that will live in Infamy. All reminders of human time passages and passings away in preparation for the Winter white blanket to lay.

<u>On Thought Control</u> 09/22/2024 02:19 PM

Closed minds see what they want. Open minds see what they can. Wise minds see what can be.

<u>On Beauty Meanings</u> 09/22/2024 02:28 PM

It was a beautiful wedding. It was a beautiful life.

It was a beautiful death. It was a beautiful strife. It was a beautiful war. It was a beautiful peace. It was a beautiful riot. It was a beautiful piece. It was a beautiful reward. It was a beautiful punishment. It was a beautiful ward. It was a beautiful … .

On Cracked Maturity 09/22/2024 03:19 PM

A human who matures into an overtly and overly class-conscious personality exhibits a true sign of a personality vulnerable. Running away from reality streams exhausting.

On Public Interactions 09/22/2024 03:31 PM

Every public endeavor attracts a public perspective reaction. Understanding helps to sort out the messes humans create.

On Politics Speak 09/22/2024 03:38 PM

An uttered dangling "this" has ruined many aspirations of an attempted empire exchange.

On Quiet Desperation 09/22/2024 06:44 PM

At the moment of any birth, desperation begins a long march.

On Morale Resurrection 09/22/2024 09:13 PM

A life of terrible moments can be rescued but not completely resurrected. Too many broken parts remain as memory torments.

<u>On Doing Randoms</u> 09/22/2024 09:23 PM

Unfortunately, too many people know what they are doing and do it anyway.

<u>Technology Hope Scales</u> 09/22/2024 10:26 PM

With technology it often feels like living on a hope scale. Never break down. Less than likely breakdown. Maybe breakdown. More than likely breakdown. Hope drains eternal, like a leaky water pipe. Total breakdown. Ugh hell level awaits.

<u>On Why</u> 09/23/2024 02:16 AM

What is this life journey? Why was I given a ticket to it? Just what is it about? The odds are good some of the aborted lives might have helped to unravel the planet earth societal mess. "It" is about. But why?

<u>On Human Species Evolutionary Needs</u> 09/23/2024 03:25 AM

Homo sapiens have evolved in physique and brain

cell capacity from cave inhabitance manwoman into worldwide land-sea manwoman travelers. We evolved according to planetary biology rules. Outer space will not evolve according to extant earth rules or extant human rules.

Yes, we've adapted to and modified existence on planet earth to fit our needs, in a minuscule degree measure over 200,000 plus years, from stone pounding to intricate time and efficiency technology enhancements but outer space is many millennia's away from significant human modifications. Inhabitations of outer space regions will significantly alter our species biology. We will need to evolve from a planet earth species into a pseudo human outer space species. Homo sapiens "what" merits a too be determined answer.

There is even an unanswered question regarding whether homo sapiens evolved from outer space seeds of life that entered Earth's atmosphere randomly landing upon the planet's soil and seas, then eventually sprouting up and assisting the evolution of all life on planet Earth. We could already be the offspring of biological entities from the outer reaches of the cosmos. The human searches into outer space almost seem like an emotional response like that of an adopted child, once an adult, seeking to know their genetic origin.

When humans begin a permanent existence in the outer cosmos, they will have already started an evolution into a new species order as part human and part outer space origin hybrids. Consider also whether the many pre-homo sapiens species known to have previously existed and went extinct is a small sample of all potential humanoid clans previously extant, as many may have been obliterated in the varied climate change catastrophes dotting the planets history, from asteroid or meteor strikes to relatively fast developed changes in the atmospheric conditions creating tropical, temperate and ice age climates.

(Look for origin of sapiens, and add an outer space designation using same language model = what does sapiens mean?)

Humans will split into two species. One mainly earth bound, and the other mostly space bound. Eventually, a human child will be conceived and born in outer space. That moment will start as the mark of a new potential humanoid species. As a test of this new species in the first stages of a new life form evolution, that child must live and grown in a complete life cycle never once stepping upon earth. Such an experiment would progress gradually as outer space born children will be transported back to earth in regular cycles likely determined by age development. A most complete cycle would involve transfer of this new human/humanoid back and forth at least once a year until the end-of-life cycle. Purpose: determine viability or necessity of a hybrid earth-outer space humanoid's development biologically and physically. Studies of brain activity comparisons between solely human occupied beings (only earth-bound existence), hybrid beings (regularly transported back and forth), and solely outer space beings (only space bound) would be required. Such studies may provide significant insights to be determined.

The biology, physiology, and neural capacities and limitations need to be determined and recorded for analysis. Growth and aging cycles must be analyzed to glean similarities and differences between each of the evolved species types. Benefits and detriments of outer space travel must be assessed in order to advance space travel opportunities. For instance, is the life cycle of the human origin species affected by space travel. Similar studies and analysis must be applied to the hybrid species and the outer space species. Next, repetitive sets of male/female human, hybrid, and solely outer space born/life cycled must be studied and analyzed. One of the significant drawbacks of such studies is inherent bias. Those conducting the studies will like harbor an invisible bias towards each human/humanoid species. Bias will always be a concern as each of the three species will naturally want to discover their own strengths and weaknesses independently. This natural / nature circumstance will inevitably lead to conversations and arguments (more hopefully constructive) regarding citizenship, residency, and common law and statutory law applications or regulations applicable to each species. The entire earth code of law may need to be rewritten. Such a task may never be resolved agreeably.

Currently we don't have space colonies set up yet

either commercially built artificial, or nature built such as asteroids, meteors, planetoids, or moons. One or more of these genetic origin humans needs to test out housing mechanisms supporting each species life cycles before any valid comparison answers can be acquired. I would argue these types of living environments must be explored and tested before a trip to another planet becomes feasible, unless only a temporary stay to such a location is planned. I haven't yet covered food and water / liquid necessities just yet, but will describe a bit later.

On Something Missing

Date Time Unknown

Inhabitants of Earth live amidst a forever war in their own lands and seas, and further, from outer space projectiles creating a start, stop, start, stop evolution series of events since the planet Earth's inception.

Something was written here, but it has disappeared . . .

Farming ---

The Matrix Puzzle

--- Liquid Nourishment

An Evolution Wrinkle In Time

A Random Rogue Time Stamp

A Flip of The Page

How would these children of earth, hybrids, and outer space receive food and liquid nourishment? How would they stay physically and mentally fit? How would they be educated? Who would educate them? The home worlds of each group would involve language and vocabulary rules remarkably different. Cultures would be remarkably different.

All of these necessaries would necessarily be debated and decided by the fathers and mothers of each species grouping. I dissect briefly one of the above aspects. Education.

First presume, and this is a big presumption, the species groupings all speak the same language, which moves us into the education process. The usual basics of reading, writing, and arithmetic would be necessary, but the science, sociology, and geography studies would take several years to be learned presuming the teachers are capable of adequately communicating the lessons. Initial outer space colonies would not be enabled to accommodate certain knowledge groups in person due to an inability to construct domains large enough to accommodate the needed education groups plus inhabitants. Likely, the educational needs would be addressed by Earth-bound teachers using known earth communication methods for the "to and from" outer space inhabitants digestion. Audio-visual transmissions needed.

Eventually job categories would need replacement. Mainly in the astronaut training categories. To conserve space in the manufactured living environment, individual astronauts would need training and skills to fulfill multiple roles of science, medical, and spacecraft technology maintenance roles. Robotic assistance likely needed for many maintenance issues. It would be interesting if self-healing structural technology could be developed. You've noticed by now that my mind has tapped into numerous science fiction novels, novellas, and short stories addressing all of these issues in detail.

One more issue. Then my escape from this portion of the story. Farming, seeds and seed growth and maintenance, a viable and reproducible water production and maintenance system, greenhouses structures plus the maintenance conditions, soil, nutrients, vitamin supplements, medicinal drug products are all considerations for extremely long-term outer space housing survival of the inhabitants. Why? Health, bone structure, weight, space effects on the human nervous system, brain activity alteration, and much more to consider.

For now, I must cease working on these considerations as volumes upon volumes of science and fantasy books have already been written filled with such ruminations. So, I abandon this laymen's puzzle solving scrutiny effort. Too many pieces of it remain to be discovered. Estimated time frame of new human branch of species development is two generations from now. I won't be around by then, so just saying "Welcome, Adam OSH1 or Eve OSH1."

(OSH = Outer Space Human)

On Salivation 09/23/2024 02:35 PM

The purpose of human animal and other creature salivation depends on the needs of the orifice location.

On Toilet Paper 09/23/2024 02:39 PM

Buy the more expensive two-ply toilet paper. Saves time and the body will say “thank you”.

On Journalism Poop 09/23/2024 03:47 PM

“Listen to what these experts say”. If the referred to experts are not named to assist credibility assessments of intellectual cogency, then the story is journalism poop. Flush.

On Spoiled Reality 09/23/2024 06:21 PM

Reality doesn’t like to be ignored. It hovers above any professed need for tolerance.

On Ruinous Fantasy 09/23/2024 07:37 PM

As a youth it was easy to surmise that truth spoke like a Walt Disney fantasy character. We learned fantasy truth was fantasy. Took us a while to dissociate our minds from such strangled in the translation truth. Really, a school lesson applicable. When the magic dies, born realities rise.

On Down Memory Lane 04/26/2022 02:11 AM

Stubbed big toe on a bed frame leg which sent my memory back in time: "The major media and Big Tech outlets try to convince us that we are lost without them, yet still some of them communicate in an absolvable fashion, washing sins away lightly during an early spring thunder storm. Perhaps it's a good societal mask that necessarily becomes our shield. Always a medieval sword versus shield world, it seems." – Mike Gutowski

On Choice 09/24/2024 04:14 AM

"The one thing you can't take away from me is the way I choose to respond to what you do to me. The last of one's freedoms is to choose one's attitude in any given circumstance." – Victor E. Frankl, Austrian neurologist, psychologist, philosopher, and Holocaust survivor

On Moments Austere 09/24/2024 12:43 PM

There is nothing sacred except by choice.

On A Moments Haunting 09/24/2024 01:05 PM

Forgiveness is a choice and not a requirement.

__On Self-Control__ 09/24/2024 01:11 PM

Growth includes mastering and metering control of desires. When that control is not achieved then a quicker path to failure has been found.

__On a Recent Insect Dream__ 09/24/2024 01:42 PM

Recently I dreamt about two blue wasps. I'm unsure whether they actually exist. The hues of these wasps wound around it like non-blue (yellow and black) wasp coatings. This dream event happened during an Uber assisted auto trip to a neighborhood grocery store. Upon arriving at my destination and before exiting the vehicle, I turned to unlatch the seatbelt clip and noticed some motion behind me which merited further observation. Free from the seat belt's hold, I looked out the rear window and that's where the blue wasp haunting commenced.

Each wasp measured medium in size compared to the awake days sizes I had noticed. The moved away from each other in a slow and steady line, wings fluttering noticeably visible almost down to the wing edges. A purpose of protecting that space of atmosphere seemed evident. For what protection purpose unknown. Then a dark curtain fell upon the dream screen, and I awoke to start my non-dream portion of the day.

Later during this day, I flipped on the Vizio screen and skipped through some channels until I came across former President Trump giving a political speech. The lower edge banner on the screen noted "Economic Policy Speech in Savannah, Georgia". Rumination required whether the blue wasps dream and the Trump speech beckoned a connection. Blue wasps moving away from each other slowly while Trump's speech encompassed a goal of humans coming closer together regarding the country's economic issues.

On Tech Whammy 09/24/2024 02:24 PM

The control of data is everything for Big Tech. They are Barbarians at the AI gate. It's their thing.

On Necessary Times 09/24/2024 02:41 PM

While parked on the toilet or necessary, many memories can intercede and intrude amongst the larger moments of body refuse removal and disposal. Wondering how many book themes or character narratives emanated forth during this somewhat time-consuming essential moment.

On Political Evolution 09/24/2024 04:15 PM Marxists and socialists hide in the Democrat party like roaches under the kitchen sink cabinet.

On Journalism Dead On Arrival 09/24/2024 04:29 PM

By and large the Journalism Industry has regularly chosen sides politically while harboring a mind-boggling passion for such a pursuit. Their viability of reliable intellectual transportation has halted more than a wheel-less auto parked upon cinder blocks. No where to go and no place to hide. Their wheels and rims have been heisted neatly and properly.

On Voter Gaps 09/24/2024 07:41 PM

I find it less than humorous when journalists mention a political “enthusiasm gap”. More accurately it should be called a “cultural brainwashing gap”.

On Roads Less Travelled 09/24/2024 08:39 PM

The road less travelled is less travelled for a reason.

It's the harshest path to reality and freedom.

On Politician Reflections 09/25/2024 07:56 PM

When will citizens realize that elected politicians are not heroes. Once in office, they morph into their true shrewd shrew selves, and not one much appreciated by the reflection of any mirror perspective. To see them as they truly are evokes a miserable sense of doom. Especially when they herd together.

On Politician Attributes 09/25/2024 07:58 PM

Politicians avoid "yes" or "no" answers to questions they don't like as if they are hiding from the spread of a deadly plague virus. Shame is no mystery to them.

On Democracy Meaning 09/25/2024 08:04 PM

The modern-day definition of democracy is no different than the definitions of Marxism and Communism. These words cry now synonymous with similar meanings.

On Vaccine Politization 09/25/2024 08:50 PM

The meanings of vaccines have been morphed into

dystopian world citizen control mechanisms.

On Elitest Perspectives 09/25/2024 09:34 PM

Seriously, some of the elitest humans live in a different world, so to them, ours looks a bit shitty. Yes, they live duped, and they deserve the benefits of living duped. One of those benefits is living clueless.

On Communication Old School 09/25/2024 09:56 PM

Whomever controls the microphone controls the message.

On Political Change 09/25/2024 10:42 PM

It could be posed that the systematic destruction of this country is complete and only the planning of a parade for a new country has not yet been completed. This "new" lives intentionally invisible to the general public.

On Big Tech Evolution 09/25/2024 10:54 AM

Big Tech isn't helping us. It is enslaving us. They've learned the politician system of management quite well.

<u>On "Fair Share" Math</u> 09/24/2024 11:03 PM

Trusting a politicians definition of Fair is like trusting a grizzly bear to eat only part of their prey.

<u>On Crazy World</u> 09/25/2024 11:13 PM

After candidate Trump was first elected President, Hollywood celebs publicly spouted death threats. Now, the Biden-Harris administration spouts the same types of threats.

Wisdomish Pukes

<u>On Evolution More</u> 09/26/2024 01:32 AM

Mother fuckers have more recently emigrated to the dystopian Provence of Gender Equity.

<u>On Life Lessons</u> 09/26/2024 01:37 AM

No one stays young forever. Time use matters.

<u>On Big Tech Math</u> 09/26/2024 01:43 AM

The calculations of Big Tech influence on generations of the world populace are palpable. What started out as a promising knowledge sharing tool has progressed into a maze of propaganda pushes timely instituted as a sway in mind thinking. The proverbial Genie escaped from the mythical bottle and evolved into an inhabitant of Pandora's box. Now the most prominent and lazy source of knowledge, there is no turning back against the Big Tech created tide. All bridges to the past have been burned. The past is now easily corrupted or erased by the turn of a switch. Science fiction and dystopian fantasy authors have deftly shown the prophetic modus operandi.

On Sheeple 09/26/2024 09:19 PM

A government that treats citizens as sheep is a pack of wolves.

On New World Order 09/27/2024 01:08 AM

The twenty-first century sure is bizzarro world.

On Life's Calculations 09/27/2024 03:24 AM

Just when life seems all figured out, some part of the equation shifts radically.

On Paths Planned and Fated 09/27/2024 04:23 AM

What can be imagined tests reality ropes. Hopes can only be realized by planning, preparing, and learning along life's rocky roads whether chosen or chanced. There is a reason, and perhaps one fortunate, for birth of our existence. Fate be damned.

<u>On Earth Peace</u> 09/27/2024 04:32 AM

If a planet of peace and human tranquility can be achieved, why has the most sentient beast placed upon it still not accepted such an achievable existence condition? Perhaps humans are not qualified worthy for such an employment responsibility. We still live amongst each other like pre-history tribes.

<u>On Statist Systems</u> 09/27/2024 04:39 AM

We sought knowledge to improve the earth condition. Or, so we said, taught, touted, marketed, profited from. We've only succeeded in creating a more sophisticated method of chaining ourselves along the links of prejudice and hatred. We regularly kick the hornets' nest thinking our holier than thou perspectives will make us immune to the impending chaotic stings. That road seems to illustrate it has no end in sight. Repair the road.

<u>On Law and Social Order</u> 09/27/2024 04:45 AM

One too many second chances inevitably leads to the murder of innocence.

On Morality 09/27/2024 04:47 AM

There is no mercy in misery.

On Political Cooking 09/27/2024 04:48 AM

Word salads do not a sentient meal make. Fire the chef.

On Deflation of Humane Contact 09/27/2024 04:57 AM

The most common characteristic of 21st century humans is how frequently they tend to an effort at glorifying humaneness. Debasement of humane decorum now rules all communication efforts.

On Word Relevance and Application 09/27/2024 04:58 AM

Freedom is just a word. The word's meaning has left town and remains unable to be found.

On Daily Dirty Function Moments 09/27/2024 05:10 AM

An average human day on planet Earth involves washing away physically and mentally the varied and many times predictable moments of misery required to function effectively and efficiently, from awaking to sleeping moments, and hurry scurry moments in between. These moments could be more specifically delineated but every reader or listener of these words can make connections to these life moments and experiences derived therefrom to find suitable and applicable examples. A reluctance to identify any specific examples rules this moments consciousness.

<u>On Cosmetic Cosmology</u> 09/27/2024 01:54 PM

A lipstick case speaks all we need to know about the human animal.

<u>On Random Feels</u> 09/27/2024 02:22 PM

Live and let die. Pie in the sky. Wonders why. Let children cry. Say goodbye. No need to try. Search for why. Seek and pry. The best lie. McDonald's fry. Two-ply dry. Crazy nigh. Kitty shy. Walk on by.

Caitie clack Jack. Fake money frack. Walking back. Running stack. Playing flack. Praying pack. Memory track. Sidewalk crack. Never look wack. Bingo clack. Murmurs ack. Orchestral hack.

Terrestrial sack. Dull tack. Misfortune knack. Energy lack. Painted black. Syrup slack. Turkey quack. Voting rack.

Terrible twos. Kanga hues. Happy ruse. Hopeful news. Sports boos. Quenchable booze. Haunting coos. Turgid cues. Past-time dues. Plaintive moos. Humanoid zoos. Arid loos. Unwanted news. Preferred clues. Holey shoes. Bedtime blues. Secretive shoos. Telegraphed trues. Nasty sues. Brazen chews. Failed flews. Neat flues. Taunted brews. Fractured woos.

<u>On Politics Sours</u> 09/27/2024 04:04 PM

How do we like our socialism served? Violent as hell's flowers, apparently. Do they have a policy plan that doesn't kill us?

<u>On Secret Immigration Flights</u> 09/27/2024 04:08 PM

The early hours of day immigration, pre-dawn morning, amply demonstrates the vial, diabolical, degenerate, monstrous machinations of the country's management administration. Bastards and bitches of death they are. Corrupt as all hell. Easily comparable to a terrorist organization in action. Count the crooks. Count the murders. Meanwhile, the politicians fatten their bank accounts. Ack! Ugh!

<u>On Primary Misery Origins</u> 09/27/2024 04:25 PM

Our politicians and their friends get richer while the citizens get poorer. What's wrong with this picture?

<u>On Liar Grazing</u> 09/27/2024 04:29 PM

Liars are plyers of misery.

<u>On Word Connections and Intersections</u> 09/27/2024 04:38 PM

The time or circumstances of word usage hinges upon the moment's necessity. Too many bores and endangers. Too few confuses and creates sores of error.

<u>On Human Tastes Flawed</u> 09/27/2024 04:46 PM

Many politicians are hated for their obvious, unprosecuted corruption, and still, favored by those many citizens who benefit from it. Some politicians are hated for their honesty and verbal candor. These are the ones targeted by the administrative state for expulsion or prosecution. We live in a crazy world.

<u>On Human Natures</u> 09/27/2024 04:54 PM

Humans being human has evolved as an existence catastrophe. Humans being humane fortunately still exists.

<u>On Mind Blinks</u> 09/27/2024 05:55 PM

"Unlimited power in the hands of limited people always leads to cruelty." – Aleksandr Solzhenitsyn (Source: Facebook – Shadows Within My Mind)

<u>On Politics Transactions</u> 09/27/2024 09:34 PM

Where the money goes is where the corruption flows.

<u>On Politics Games</u> 09/27/2024 10:29 PM

Politicians are so corrupt. How corrupt are they? They can steal anything they want without fear of prosecution, as long as they tow the party line.

<u>On Creativity Tools</u> 09/28/2024 03:15 AM

The greater the horsepower of an imagination engine, the greater a chance of nonsense emanated exhaust.

On Political Crimes 09/28/2024 04:08 PM

For the first time in USA history, the number of registered voter Republicans exceeds the number of Democrats voter registrations. Conveniently for Democratic Party members, Democrats control the Biden-Harris administration. Biden-Harris, upon entry to the White House on day one, instituted a new voter recruitment scheme by opening the country borders and then proceeded to invite in anyone and everyone from other countries into the USA, and then intentionally improperly vetted the requirements of these immigrants for admission into the country. Many of them are not vetted for occupational or social needs enhancement which is the generally accepted reason for admission of new immigrants. The numbers entered are staggering, somewhere between fifteen million to twenty million in less than four years.

Predictably, the lax vetting process permitted entry of thousands upon thousands of criminals who were tossed out of their previous residence countries, many from jails were they were serving an existing prison sentence for murder, rape, child abuse and child trafficking, and other heinous crimes. The Democrat Party administration didn't care. They were looking to increase their voter numbers. Risked life and limb of legal citizens. Recently it was reported that the Biden-Harris administration has fast-tracked the new citizen registration process. There could be only one reason for such a scheme. To gain new voters for election needs of the Party.

The immediate result of the skewed and corrupt immigration process is a major increase in nationwide criminal activities which have resulted in murders and rapes of USA current residents. In addition, drug traffickers have taken over small towns and small cities as means to traffic drugs and sex workers.

Ask yourself this question: what has the Democrat Party in the USA become? Well, to find the answer, read the above factually accurate circumstances outlined briefly above. Read it a few times if necessary. Our once great nation is being negatively exploited at the whim of corrupt politicians and their government agency and contracted workers organizations. Our country now exists in the end stages of not just a republic, but also the end stages of a democracy.

The media outlets controlled by the Democratic Party don't report these truths easily obtained and realized by the average citizen. Most of the outlets answer to the Democratic Party.

Essentially, the Party has returned to its slavery roots. Their actions are a means to control citizens. Such control has existed since the time of the Democratic Pary founding of the Ku Klux Klan organization whose intentions were to control the populace using violence. You will find many definitions of the Klan, most of them altered historically for a good conspicuous reason. They were founded in the southern States and their intent was to resist against Republican rule after the Civil War ended. Some of the modern-day definitions describe them as "right wing". That definition is a clear misrepresentation intended to confuse citizens. Their intention was to revolt by any means necessary against a government controlled by the Republican Party at the time.

Sound familiar? Democrat Presidential candidate

Harris can be seen on video touting a necessity for similar violent criminal actions as means to control the parts of the populace who disagree with her concept of a changed societal structure. Her vision of management for the country involves principles similar to the principles of the Ku Klux Klan (a Democrat Party "solution" at the time). Control by force, or else. Her Vice-Presidential candidate is an avowed socialist. Starting to click?

Harris has been described as a leftist. Her actions in the past speak to such a description. Her VP candidate ruling principles are ensconced in socialism. He, too, has explicitly stated so. Their schemes amount to a "final solution" for the Republican problem. (See Democrat Party and Joe Biden and propaganda media references available on-line also proposing a "final solution" for that pesky Republican Party problem.)

Rimtoad 09/28/2024 07:33 PM

(Brief Short Story) (Origin idea 03/14/2024, 10:31 AM, initial outline phase. Below is what the initial idea has become as translated into story lines.)

Ribbit.

A human approached. He perched on a slimy rock which jutted up enough above the water's line top. No sun just yet showed itself, so he thought he would wait a while for it, and laze about on the rock for a short nap. No dangers struck an awareness in his body or senses. Just another lazy day of tongue flick as the flying tiny species of insects hovering about and above the water line not too far from the shore line.

Muddy Creek had been his home and that of his family for generations, or at least since yesterday, he wasn't sure. His memory generally worked in brief time spans. He appreciated time as the wait for a next meal. A beautiful laze it had become after a bit. Quiet except for the creek worlds innate soundings. "Oh, what mysteries to be solved today", his mind asked.

A clanky bark sound didn't alarm him. The sound meant Park Ranger had just arrived and wished to stroll around to spy whether creek world was still doing what it was supposed to do, whatever that was. He knew it as home and that's all that really mattered. Park Rangers steps grew louder. Meant she was approaching his rock area, or at least the rock he had claimed today, temporarily. Her movement and mouth sounds drew closer. Maybe an inspection necessary, or a moment to say hello.

"Hello, Rimtoad," her voice sang. (Her aroma alerted to a potential mating moment, at the proper time of the season. Perhaps these grand visions streamed as fantasy bytes.) He liked the sound of her voice. Not the typical croak he had been accustomed to. A nice air strum. She called out "New". He didn't know New. Never met New. Wondered if she would elaborate. Not sure if New was good or bad. She observed at him while he rested on the creek rock of his choice and favor. Observation scared him. She didn't attack him. Comforting circumstance of chance in creek lands.

She wasn't an owl, or she'd be darting at him with those stone glaring eyes. The owl wings alone, when spread, struck fear in creek land. No. She wasn't an owl. Her aroma still created distraction thoughts. A weapon? Dive time? The water would protect him if he could get deep enough. But the rock calls forth a noble's day comfort unforgettable, almost acting like an entrapment of mind. Or maybe a magnet of doom. He must move his head to spy whether hungry others approached, but then such a movement would exude fear, and maybe tempt a more immediate attack from others.

Snazzy outfit, too, she wore today. A pretty skin cover. He often wondered if he would ever find one like hers. She did once arrive out of the normal visit time range wearing a different skin. Maybe to relax. Or maybe she hadn't finished cleaning that skin yet. He noticed the lack of a tiny tin gleam on her skin cover below her head near one of her leg extensions. No sun yet to make it gleam or reflect at him. Once she bent down close to him, at the edge of the shore line, and he saw the brim of another skin near the mouth. Took him a while to realize it was him reflecting back as his eye. "Not too bad of a look," he thought. Too early for the lady toads to appear. Wouldn't be for at least many more eats time passings. Anyway, his full light-blue colors had not yet grown upon his skin. Mating time not yet signaled by the creek creatures.

Then he noticed hair, like the possums hair, when she removed her cap to scratch around at the hair a bit. He liked that cap. It had a picture of him on it, or at least what looked a bit like his water reflection.

Then, something happened. Park Ranger snapped her face viewers, eyes, towards a place farther down the creek line. He wanted to look but didn't want to disturb his laze. A wonder, like that of the hungry racoon, appeared on Park Ranger's face. It was time for something. Or maybe something happened that it was not time for. Or maybe something happened unexpectedly. Park Ranger's look seemed funny to him. She walked towards the sound, making mud squishing sounds.

Now he wanted to move over to the squishy mud. He knew how good it would feel on his warty skin, all pillowy and serene of comfort. He adjusted his body towards her movements and noticed at a distance, just a short distance, a slowly moving fog blanket. "Uh oh," he thought. Too early for fog. An adventure approaches. Dangerous or serene? Park Ranger seems to want a know about it.

Rimtoad tried to explain to himself what events were unfolding regarding the movement of the fog blanket, towards him and his seeming new friend, but remained unable to capture thought words to describe the happenings. “Eerie, unusual, never seen a fog like this one. Darker than light. Something moving inside it, like goldfish just below the creek water surface, but goldfish don’t hide in the fog of air.” He wanted to shout at Park Ranger to stay away. A loud croak sufficed, and she stopped moving towards physical contact, then remained at a safe owls observation distance. Oddly, it was too early in the evening for owls, possums, and furries, yet they seemed drawn to the fog. Scary.

An audience now had gathered around the fog boundaries. Some of them disappeared into it. No intelligible sounds emanated afterwords, at least not of a common language nature. More like a bubbling or gurgling, like fish talk or swamp creature lingo. Along the tree line of each side of the creek, the tapping’s and trappings of avian life ceased sounding out. A scary foreboding of ill intent alerted Rimtoad slowly, but increased in frequency the closer the dark fog ventured. Even Park Ranger had to stop and merely stare.

Her body began a shake, almost like a mating dance

type of movement. He, too, began the dance, but not in a mating manner. In the fear manner. The fog had achieved the mission. Became a bubble of darkness around all it encountered. An early evening curtain of origin unknown.

Eventually, after encountering the strange fog, while still interred by the airs of it, he and the Park Ranger became absorbed into each other. When their convergence ended, and after the fog disappeared, each noticed strange changes. They each gained perspective of a more subtle nature than their individual birth species individually had acquired.

He can walk using the legs of the Park Ranger and see through her eyes. Her appetite is somewhat like his, wanting insects and bugs to eat. The Park Ranger still controlled most physical movements but he somewhat controlled dietary needs. Parts of her evolved to look like him such as feet, hands that still have fingers but are webbed, and she has warts on her back. He liked the way she looks. She is horrified how she looks now.

A physical meeting has happened intimately.

There's a bit of sliminess to her skin. Combined together they present a Jim Henson's Muppets type of physiology. He tries to communicate with her, but his sentience is buried inside her subconscious. Her emotions and physical needs are confusing to his life's essence experience.

He sees things about her. He enjoys what she eats. It's called a vegan diet. Easy for him to digest and very tasty. He wonders how such descriptive words enter his mind. That he even wonders is confusing.

Because of her appearance she is unable to find a mating partner, but he is quite pleasured during her masturbation moments. He even thought he would explode during the first such orgasmic experience, and was quite happy how calm and serene he felt afterward. She ended up buying an adjustable bed and set it on super firm. He liked that feeling, almost like sun bathing on the creek rocks. The humans didn't know her true beauty.

When she started talking about shoes he became scared. "What are shoes? Why do I have to put them on my body?" Then she started talking about seeing a doctor. Sounded scary. "What's a doctor?"

Is that another Park Ranger?"

Her sometimes response to his thoughts was verbally rendered as "I suppose". He thought such a response was better than nothing. A lessor of mysteries.

Still, hours to go before the next adventure venture. Too much or too little a time distance depends. On what such time depends he wasn't certain. Tis better to think of the future than to live it Now, sucking up its potential in trivial moments. Of course, one large moment is usually created in such a manner. Took days to find his favorite resting rock place. Now the needs of it faded in memory. Just a souvenir of past existence moments.

Her mind carried, stashed away, many such souvenirs. Too many for his mind to appreciate. Still, insights gained by seminal means and measures.

She seemed to enjoy rainy day mud flops, as he so much did. Their singular connection to the past rubbed off upon each other lyrical. Poetic. Experiences long overdue but not lost in mindsets.

Sometimes her thoughts, particularly regarding physical mating rituals, disturbed him. Before physical conjunction of their bodies such an issue never posed questions. The fog experience has changed all of those moments. He searched for better thoughts of these new realizations. Found one. A lick upon a spicey plant leaf. Dizzying, but predisposed a content rock laze. Danger poked at his mind as an unsafe sketchy place of his former nature landscape. Such dangers he had not faced in the past, despite their apparent existence. A greater awareness of life stung at his new brain. He began to miss his earlier days of ignorance about such harms. The owl preyed in darkness. Now, the owl preys at all times in his mind.

Such of her imagination memories flooded into his mind randomly. He never liked surprises. He deeply missed his wetted creek rock. He'd give himself an explanation for how he now felt, but survival thoughts necessarily interceded.

For his existence is now solely about capture of one more moment. An extended tongue flick at insects moments. And there are many more moments he desires to capture. The end? There's something not right here, he supposed. The light brown evening skylight of creek world, he missed.

Ribbit.

(Research notes: Minkowski space time; Readers Digest: 13 Small Habits That Actually … About Your Personality, and 11 Subtle Signs You're More Perceptive Than You Give Yourself Credit For; Smithsonian Magazine: hybrid animals, parthenogenesis = a type of asexual reproduction akin to cloning that's performed by some fish, reptiles, and birds; see also cross breeds of Neanderthals and Homo sapiens)

<u>On Political Strategy</u> 09/29/2024 06:12 PM

Politics and their politicians exude engine-like policies that break down regularly at the drop of a hat. Too much maintenance costs required. Or is such a circumstance planned obsolescence?

<u>On Political Infighting</u> 09/29/2024 06:17 PM

Politics is a philosophy which advocates crushing the adversary with any rocks available.

<u>On Immigration Schemes</u> 09/29/2024 06:23 PM

Under the dictatorial rule of the Biden-Harris administration, immigration has become a weapon of totalitarian citizen control.

On Varied Evolutions 09/29/2024 06:43 PM

Socially, this 21st century hoax form of existence has far exceeded any other existence form during human evolution history.

On Election Hopes 09/29/2024 07:20 PM

May the political party less adept at cheating win. That circumstance would certainly act as a kick in the head and temporary knock down of the elites.

On Treason 09/30/2024 12:27 AM

A treason of any other name, such as "Arming the Enemy of All Human Kind", is still treason.

On A Life's Philosophy 09/30/2024 12:49 AM

Somewhere between uncontrollable dreams and stubborn realities exists a plain of realization left to be explored for as long as a life remains sentient. To the extent this plain is probed, travelled, depends on life meaning goals intended, whatever and wherever such destinations are sought.

Along the way of this path, only the possessor of such an exploration mindset can suffer and attempt control of the wild stallion or hooked tarpon it is. Wear such a mindset like a real pursuit or "realsuit". Such efforts lead to a marvelous suite of understanding, although the travel effort screams pricey exhausting. Be ready to mock truth, then discover human reality.

Realsuit = mockism (realizing the living mind of life mocks the effort regularly)

Philosophy by Questions 09/30/2024 01:10 AM

Question what hurts. Then make it stop. Find a plan conventionally moral, or risk inviting more hurt. Find a battle? Or happen upon one in progress? Choose a sensible, rational, survivable path mentally and physically in order to outlast the machinations of the problem's persistence in creation of negative exploitation. Such potential solutions help to reap the economic and life sustaining benefit of employment survival and relationship longevity.

A solution sensible and sustainable can be found if sufficient time is spent on a plan process. Be prepared for a necessity to dodge and parry emotionally, then revise the planned strategy accordingly. Don't become a dog chasing its own tail.

On the Meaning of Life: Reality Fogs 09/30/2024 01:21 PM

To love is to live. Then and only then, the feeling of life merges into a fog of a forever series of moments valuable. Love feeds love itself. Love heals love itself. Love desires love. It is a give and take equation. A theory of life relativity.

To hate is a temporary emotional moment which then bumps into other emotional moments that fortunately side track and somewhat diffuse the hate energy momentums. (I'll forgo a physics equation example. Not sentient enough to expound upon one.) Drugs usage, alcohol abuses, life's frustrations whether ignited by oneself or someone else, abuse imposed by others or by accidental or unfortunate circumstances serve as fuels burning hate fires of the mind and mental state.

A balance will sometimes emerge esthetically along

the love-hate scales. An effort should be made daily to at least balance those scales, mindful of self-inflicted barriers previously experienced. Mental, physical, and intellectual wounds are more likely to be recalled, then audibly railed out against nearby innocents, effectively ruining in the future any opportunity for reasonably fair commiseration processes regarding any issue.

Care to love as means to quell the ravages of hate. Emotional blinds and distractions sour and dim perspective. Dimmed perspectives cause injury to the self, familial, and social contacts. Salient perspectives enhance such contacts. The grease that keeps the love-hate scale at least minimally balanced is intuitive understanding.

Understanding and misunderstanding are twin thought relatives. A fair and balanced human is expected to know such relationships and how they operate in daily life. Don't choose a battle which can't be won. Don't seek battle. Unnecessary drains of energy useful for more important purposes is always a risk. A tired mind leads to tiring bouts. The mind makes no sound racket except in the head of the mind holder. The mind holder is responsible for adjusting the sound dial.

Lesser sentient creatures such as dogs and cats can assist humans in the betterment of understanding life's balance. Such little creatures are adept at living a life of practicality. They tend to their needs and family needs daily. They do sometimes make mistakes, from a human perspective, while learning the rules of the human household which they occupy. They possess a need for comradery and single purpose. In essence, humans, dogs, and cats are capable of teaching each other the benefits of amicable co-habitation.

A miracle? No. It is what the meaning of life is all about. (I've always been somewhat teary eyed about this self-revelation. A too often reminder by necessity of this realization permits droplets of memory thanks.) Pass the time offered by the status of existence by pursuing a productive existence. Every community of creatures, humans or otherwise creatures upon this good in sustainable sustenance quirks, continues to live and survive under such rules and expectations.

There is no purpose of survival except to survive.

A search for a reason why becomes almost irrelevant. Such irrelevance dismisses the search for relevance. A relevance will naturally evolve upon actions the individual human chooses to make. Good choices increase the possibilities of enhanced existence opportunities. Bad choices tip the scale in the opposite direction. These choices share the same moment in time. Birth upon the planet, no matter where, when, or how it occurs. As long as a breath remains, the opportunity to balance the humanity scales remains. Only aging physiologically, and environmental conditions can then alter a free state of compatibility and cooperation. A seminal peace possibility.

Unfortunately, after the birth of the first humanoid creature millions of years ago, no such seminal, contiguous worldwide essence of peace has ever been achieved. It is too early to abandon the search for the pursuit and completion of such a goal. The current existing humans and creatures can yet still make it happen. I've resisted the instincts and intellectual conclusions my mind wishes to believe. It is a resistance necessary to proceed.

A Good Place for a Temporary Ending

True Factoid Ending 09/30/2024 02:22 PM

It is a reasonable speculation to seriously consider whether the United States of America, China, Iran, North Korea, Russia, Mexico, Canada, Great Britain, Germany, France and a few European Union leaders are allied and actively plotting a New World Order which puts Elites First, and enslaves all other humans on this planet.

On Taxation 10/01/2024 12:47 PM

Taxes are implemented as a form of citizen slavery.

On Enemies Domestic 10/01/2024 01:30 PM

For the USA citizen, like in many countries, their biggest enemy is the government hired to rule over them.

On Stimulations 10/01/2024 01:34 PM

Energy begets energy. Sloth begets sloth.

On Lying Consciously 10/01/2024 07:18 PM

Lying regularly is more than a lifestyle. It is a specific choice. It is a significant sign of intellectual immaturity.

On Religion Management 10/01/2024 10:24 PM

Religion is a time-tested theory poorly implemented in reality. I blame human management.

On Choice Parameters 10/02/2024 03:13 PM

Every human choice is political. By political I mean the choice has a beginning place, trial and error phase, and a conclusion phase. These phases work like a three-ring circus. A somewhat chaos by design, leading to a contemplation when off stage regarding the benefits and detriments of utilized action moments.

On the End Line (00/00/0000) (00:00)

What the near future holds is only a tentatively planned guess. Sometimes a well-planned guess, also called a goal. What the distant future holds is an educated speculation. Perhaps self-consulting with the writings of science fiction and dystopian fantasy authors and philosophers is helpful.

The A Dios End

Reviews appreciated.

Books by Mike Gutowski

(available on Amazon.com

as paperback and e-book):

Cratch

Time for the Dead: Zombies-A Love Story

Ariadne

Misfortunes Of Mister Knack

Seventh Ratica

According To Helen

Miserations

www.ingramcontent.com/pod-product-compliance
Lightning Source LLC
Chambersburg PA
CBHW072138300726
48975CB00003B/1106
* 9 7 9 8 9 8 7 3 4 3 3 2 6 *